"frankly TWISTED": THE LOST FILES

Table of Contents

"frankly TWISTED": THE LOST FILES

by: Kevin Eleven

Illustrations by: Alton Taylor

www.floweredconcrete.net (Official)
www.floweredconcrete.com (Blog)
www.facebook.com/FloweredConcrete
www.twitter.com/floweredlit
www.instagram.com/floweredconcrete
www.youtube.com/FloweredConcrete
www.plus.google.com/+FloweredConcrete

Stay up-to-date with the author and as well as his latest news regarding his writing by visiting his website at:
www.kevinanglade.com

Follow the author on twitter and instagram: @velevek

www.twitter.com/velevek
www.instagram.com/velevek

For bookings, readings, signings, concerns, or general inquiries regarding the work or the author in general, please be sure to e-mail him at: kevinanglade@gmail.com

 For press: floweredconcrete@gmail.com

ISBN-13: 978-0692408391 (Flowered Concrete)

ISBN-10: 0692408398

First Print Edition: July 2015

"Dedication"

"This is dedicated to anyone with a dream, and the realization of what following it means..." - Logic

BOOK TWO

Many often think that they know the characters and as well as motives behind Brooklyn's own 23rd precinct. Well the fact of the matter is that they don't as detectives find that scratching your head may be the key to figuring out where exactly it could have all went wrong. Moreover, this just so happens to be the dilemma of Parkside Avenue's finest as they now find themselves entangled within a twisted end at every single corner. However, what they haven't realized is that someone amongst their own ranks has been leading them astray and is the cause of them backtracking as a result.

Episode 1:

"Chauncey's Conclusion"

"Prisoner 4624931! Prisoner 4624931! Prisoner 4624…man, don't make me call your number again!! Get your ass up in here," yelled the corrections officer.

"Damn, why the hell are you yelling for homie?! I already ate my dinner," said the young man with an afro and orange prison jumpsuit.

When looking at the young man, there was no doubt that he was barely over twenty. He had dark brown eyes and very thin eyebrows. His afro had a pick that remained fixed within the rear of his head. As he walked towards the corrections officer, it was obvious that he had a sense of laziness about him in the way that he trudged along into the cell block.

"You had me calling you too many times to count boy," said the C.O. as he surveyed the young man from top to bottom.

One look at the C.O. showed a resemblance to the black Hollywood actor Clifton Powell. He had a thick black mustache, high-top fade and a drill-sergeant demeanor to boot.

When the young prisoner didn't respond, the C.O. then said, "I should smack you upside your head right now, you know that? But lucky for you, you've got a visitor today."

The two men continued to walk down the cell block before finally making their way into the visitor's room. As they entered it, they saw many other inmates talking to people who had traveled far and wide just to see them. Some were brothers or sisters that had simply wanted to see how their younger or older siblings were holding up. Some were women who were obviously girlfriends or wives and had grown restless of not being able to be with their men. And some were mothers that were hard-working and possibly wondering where they themselves had gone wrong during the midst of their sons' childhoods.

Nevertheless, as the two men trudged on, the corrections officer eventually brought the young man over to a man seated alone at a black and battered deserted round table.

"Hell no," said the boy as he made strides to return from where he had entered.

"Nuh-uh, where do you think you're going?" said the C.O. as he grabbed the boy by his orange collar.

"Chauncey," said the man who had been at the table waiting for his arrival.

The boy named Chauncey acted as if he hadn't heard the man and tried to push his way through the C.O.

"Chauncey, SIT!" demanded the man in a much more rigid tone.

Realizing that he wouldn't be able to avoid the man who had given him orders as well as the muscular size of the C.O., he reluctantly sat down on the opposite side of the black round table.

"That's better," exclaimed the man.

One close look at the mysterious man showed him to be in his fifties. It was weird because he looked much younger from a distance. He had grizzly black hair, a dark five o'clock shadow, and a worn look that exhibited him of going through many experiences over the previous months.

"Chaunce," he said. "Hey, kiddo. How are you holding up in here?" he asked in a tender voice that had been unexpected.

"You need anything else, Frank?" asked the C.O. as he cracked his knuckles.

"No, that will be all John, thanks," replied Frank.

The C.O. named John left without another word. With his disappearance, Chauncey and the man named Frank were left alone.

"Chauncey. I know that you probably don't want to talk to me ever again and I can understand that. I blame myself for this entire mess," said Frank candidly.

Chauncey continued to look around the visitor's room as he took in the scenery of what seemed to be happy visits among the other tables and inmates.

"Chauncey. Hey, listen to me!" said Frank as he tried to keep his voice under control and at a reasonable level.

"Man, why are you here?" said Chauncey as he finally broke his silence.

"Because you're my blood and I love you. I'm going to get you out of here. I promise," said Frank.

"I've been locked up for about four months now. Someone in here told me that we're exactly a week away from July."

"Yeah," said Frank, his eyes scanning the entire room as if he were searching for words.

"So, now?" asked Chauncey in disbelief.

"What do you-?"

"I mean, NOW!" replied Chauncey with booming force.

"Hey, hey, hey, keep your voice down son," demanded Frank.

"Why is it that *now* all of a sudden you come?" asked Chauncey in a voice of disdain.

"When they found out who you exactly were, it got really hot for me on duty. Believe me, I thought about you, I really did. Non-stop to be exact. But I was under fire. The entire 23rd precinct did a background check on me. The fact that you're my nephew and that Jake Fisher ratted you out, I was under heavy investigation. How do you think it would have been perceived if I would have come to visit you?"

"I don't know. But it shows that you don't give a damn about me! You'd rather put your job first than your own nephew. How delightful," said Chauncey with obvious sarcasm.

"Boy, understand. I'm in a position to help you… I wouldn't be able to do that if I was wearing that orange jumpsuit, running around surrounded by men trying to penetrate my anus," replied Frank.

The harshness in his voice was apparent as he began to run out of patience with his nephew.

"Whatever man," said Chauncey as he removed his pick from off the back of his head and began to attack his fro.

"I see your fro is still looking good. Shit, it's looking better than ever, now that I really think about it," said Frank with a spry smile.

When he noticed that Chauncey was seriously being unresponsive he then said, "Look I'm working on a deal. A plea deal. I'm going to try and get your seven reduced to three. Hopefully with my credentials and the cases I've solved, the judge will see it my way when you go to trial and we can get you out of here."

"Does it look like I need your help? As a matter of fact, does it look like I *want* your help?"

Frank briefly scanned the visitor's room for a second time before saying, "*Yes*, you do actually."

"I'm going to do my seven and that's that! As far as I'm concerned, I don't know you," he said coldly.

"C'mon, Chauncey, don't do this please. There's no time for it," said Frank who appeared to be frustrated.

"Exactly, you're right," replied Chauncey.

"Hey, I didn't ask for you to be here. Remember what I told you a few months back? Huh? What did I say?" asked Frank as he awaited the boy's response.

Chauncey momentarily looked hard at the ceiling before answering.

"The game always one's up the score in the end," he finally said.

Frank slightly nodded his head in agreement. He was sure that his nephew had remembered the code especially since it had been his first time locked up in confinement.

"I chose this life Uncle Frank. Not you, not my father, but me. It's Chauncey Matthews' problem. Not Frank Matthews. I'll live with it, I'll deal with it and I'll die with it if I have to. I don't care. You just concentrate on trying to protect the law, even when you know you're just in it for yourself."

"Okay, Chauncey. I'll leave if that's what you want. But believe me when I say that I'm going to get you out, mark my words. And I'll be back. You're as good as my son and you know that," said Frank.

Chauncey chuckled as he finally got up and returned the rickety chair that he had been sitting on right underneath the black round table.

"That's funny," he said as he leaned into his uncle's face. "Because at one point you were as good as my father."

As he began to walk away with his back turned, it was then that another C.O. who was waiting in the wings escorted Chauncey back down the corridor and into his cell.

All Frank Matthews could do was stare at the rickety black chair that had been sitting opposite of him.

It was apparent to him that the relationship he once shared with his nephew had been changed forever.

As Matthews sat and pondered upon how he would reduce the sentence of a young man named Chauncey Matthews, never did he once think that he had spoken to his nephew for what was possibly the very last time…

Episode 2:

"A Lane of My Own"

To anyone reading this lost file, please, allow me to introduce myself. My name is Deborah Lane, a detective of the BKPD within the burglary/narcotics unit of the 23rd precinct. As I go back in time and recall this story, please be sure to bear with me, it happened almost twenty years ago. As I write this, I'm currently sitting in my home at my computer desk just jotting things down as they come. The biggest question you may be asking is *'How can a woman such as detective Lane hold her own in a field dominated by men?'* Once again, I ask that you look no further…here's my perspective on it all. I was working at the 23rd precinct for three years as a black uniformed officer before I got my first real shot. Allow me to take you all back in time…the year was 1996…

I

"Lane, did you file those transactions on the Dan Hoover case like I asked you to?" said Captain Gordon as he flipped through a stack of papers within his right hand.

"Of course I did cap," I said through clenched teeth as I bent over to tie my shoe laces while trying to keep the pen that I had been using from falling out of my mouth.

"And where's Fisher?" asked Gordon as he now maneuvered behind my desk and dropped his stack of papers upon it with a loud thud.

15

"I'm not sure, he was supposed to be back ten minutes ago," I said as I once again went to the floor to pick up some papers that had fallen suddenly out of the blue.

The moment I did this, I felt my back side begin to burn as I was sure that Captain James Gordon was staring at my rear.

Truth be told, I considered Captain Gordon to be very annoying and a bit of a creep. Whenever he was around, it was extremely hard to hold back from giving him a piece of my mind. Ever since my first day on the job, I knew that the captain had been attracted to me, but no matter how much he put himself within my presence, there would certainly be no chance of a fling or whatever thought that possibly ran across his old and creepy mind.

"Are you looking for something?" I asked as I abruptly turned around and tried to catch him in the act.

"No, not at all," he said awkwardly as he played with his tie in nervous fashion.

As I quickly made my way to the office door and opened it for fresh air, Fisher suddenly walked in with a box full of papers and a snickers bar dangling from the tip of his mouth.

"I'm back," he said as he dropped the brown cardboard box by the desk.

Fisher had on his black uniformed BKPD shirt while his officer hat was tilted to the side. He looked as if he had been pushed by an oncoming crowd.

"Where have you been Fisher?" asked Gordon as he surveyed him from top to bottom.

"I was just out during my break, when I decided to grab a snickers. And then, on my way back up here, detective Alvin wanted me to bring those files to you that you now see on the ground."

"I see," said Gordon as he gave a huge sigh. "Looks like we've got a few new cases on our hands," he said as he looked at each printed file within the box that Fisher had brought in carefully.

"Lane."

"Yeah, cap?"

"Are you ready for an important one?" he asked as he stared me right in the eye.

"Why of course," I said sharply as I quickly got up and made my way to where he had been crouching and staring at the files. Gordon swiftly reacted by closing up the box and picking it up with both hands.

"Tomorrow," he said hastily. "It's too late to divulge any of the information now. So with that being said, we'll discuss it at eight hundred hours sharp!" he said crisply before leaving the room.

"You want a ride home, Deb?" asked Fisher as he now made his way towards me and advanced so close that our noses almost touched.

"No thanks, Luke. I'm just going to train it today," I told him while looking at the office clock.

"Are you sure? You know, I don't mind," he said as he helped me put things away.

"Uh-huh. I'm sure," I told him in an adamant voice. "But thanks for the offer, anyhow," I added.

Fisher and I were most certainly the youngest two cops at the 23rd precinct. He had just turned twenty-five, while I, on the other hand, was twenty-six. We had both come a long way in the past two years within the department and yet, we still had long ways to go.

"Well, sounds cool. I guess I'll just see you tomorrow then, Deb," he said as he made strides to leave the office.

"Yep, I'll see you then," I replied as I waited for him to leave before subsequently making my exit.

||

Later on, that night, I walked into my SoHo apartment and found my fiancé Daniel Lane setting up dinner utensils at the dinner table.

We had only been together for two years but planned to be wed the following spring. He was a very attractive man that had curly brown hair, green eyes and possessed the physique of an NFL star quarterback. He was a restless and diligent working twenty-nine year old that had just started establishing himself as a promising defense attorney. As I made my way to the kitchen to wash my hands, he silently swooped me off of my feet and carried me to the dinner table. On our way there, we kissed often and passionately.

After unveiling my dish which consisted of steamed shrimp, sea-shells and as well as crab, he then said, *"Bon appetite"* in what was a terrible impersonation of a French accent.

With a forced smile, I told him, "thank you," and slowly began to eat my food.

"What's wrong?" he asked as he took a sip of the red wine in his glass.

What I truly appreciated about Daniel was that he could always sense when something was on my mind. As hard as I tried, I couldn't get anything past him.

"Nothing," I said as I forced myself to not meet his eye.

Daniel simply continued to gaze before I finally succumbed to the pressure.

"A case," I said in matter-of-fact fashion as I played with the shrimp on my plate.

"Nice!" he said, and then added, "I know you've been waiting for this for a very long time. Looks like I made dinner on a perfect night," he said as he took another sip of wine before pouring some from the bottle into my own empty glass.

"I just hope I'm ready," I told him as I felt my voice shake.

"Of course you'll be. Didn't Gordon say that you are the fastest woman in the 23rd precinct to ever achieve detective one rank status?" he asked.

"Yeah, but-"

"But, nothing, I have one hundred percent faith in you, honey. You've been a great beat cop the past few years and so now, you get the opportunity to apply it to actual cases. Trust me, you're ready," he said.

"What if I di—"

"No what ifs, deaths, nothing," he said firmly as he made his way behind me and wrapped his arms around my chest.

He then found my chin delicately with his clenched right fist and brought it up to meet his face.

"You'll be fine," he said with such passion and confidence before kissing me once again.

He then took off his shirt to reveal his nicely framed and chiseled athletic body.

"Come with me," he crooned softly as he beckoned me towards the bedroom.

As I got up to follow him, I felt my pager vibrate from within my pants. When I pulled it out to see who had paged me, I saw Fisher's number flash in a background of neon green light. As I placed the pager back into my pocket, I quickly made my way to the bedroom where Daniel had been waiting for me patiently.

III

The next day, I arrived at the 23rd precinct at eight a.m.

Gordon had told me to arrive early in order to discuss matters pertaining to the new case that I'd soon be working on.

"Good morning," he said.

"Good morning captain," we all chorused in return.

And as he walked inside of the conference room, the entire unit became silent.

"A new case," he then said, as he waved a few files that had been in his hand back and forth before finally dropping them onto the table.

"What kind?" asked a detective by the name of Travis Williams who had been sitting and listening to Gordon's every word.

"Organized crime," he replied.

Immediate chatter permeated the room as all the detectives and uniformed cops talked about what had just been mentioned amongst themselves.

"So," said Captain Gordon with such force that the chatter died down instantaneously as it had come.

"There's a mafia working out of East New York. Their leader's name is Mark Gambini. We've been trying to catch this guy for years, but for some reason, he's always managed to slither out of our grasp like the snake in the Garden of Eden.

"Gambini's currently got his hand in everything, from narcotics, casinos, strip clubs, you name it and we can bet that he and his crew are at the helm of it all. We've been getting word that he and his people have been smuggling drugs from Colombia recently."

Gordon, noticing that he had the ear of the entire department, began to pace up and down without breaking even a second's eye contact with all of his officers.

"Cocaine, heroin, opium, LSD, once again, you name it and he's got it," he said.

"Now, I want you guys to go out there and see what you can find. The man is planning on receiving his deal within the next few days and I want to make sure that we're all there to stop it," he said in a tone of finality.

"Lane, this has got your name written all over it. You've got first dibs on this one. Pick someone in whom you know will be of great assistance to this case. And as for the rest of you, you guys are to research to the best of your knowledge so that I can pass info on to Lane, here. Got it? Dismissed!"

A dozen police officers as well as detectives made their way out of the door when Gordon had clasped his big hands onto my shoulders.

"Good luck," he said.

"Sure," I responded nervously.

"And keep me posted," he urged before leaving me alone in the office.

As much as I had prayed on it, the day finally came in which I now had to prove myself. The moment I sat down at my stationed computer and began to do my research, Luke Fisher came in and sat directly across from me.

"Well?" he asked nervously.

"Yes, I got it," I said calmly as I continued working on my computer.

"That's great," he said as he sat next to me and watched what I had been doing.

"I want you to come on the case with me," I said without looking up.

"No," he said in awed disbelief with his eyes opened wide in amazement.

"Yes," I giggled.

"No way, seriously?" he asked in astonishment.

"Shut up before I change my mind," I said.

"Are you sure? What did Gordon say?"

"I haven't told him as of yet," I said casually as I began to write down some addresses on a blank sheet of paper.

"You think he'd let—"

"Look," I said as I spun my chair to meet his eye.

"You can do this. Besides, you don't want to be a uniformed cop forever, right? You're the only one in whom I've truly felt comfortable with in this place, anyway, therefore, I know that we can solve this case. And as for Gordon, don't worry about it, I'll be sure to have him see it my way."

"I guess everyone's gotta spread their wings sometimes," said Fisher in an airy voice as he fully extended his arms as if he were a plane.

Fisher and I suddenly burst out laughing. I was certain that I had picked the right person to accompany me on the case.

Later that day, Fisher and I made our way to Loon Hung. Hung's was a gigantic Chinese buffet restaurant that stood in between Eastern Parkway and Rochester Avenue. After some intensive research, I learned that Gambini and his henchman had often ate there in between their dirty work.

When we walked into the restaurant, a pretty little Chinese girl greeted our presence with a bow as she led us to the register where the food sat simmering in heat behind the counter.

"We're not here to eat little dumpling," said Fisher as he patted her head as if she were a puppy.

"Now, run along and get us whomever that runs this damn place," said Fisher as he looked at all the people that had been happily eating their food.

It had been obvious to me that for his first case, Fisher had been trying way too hard.

"But Grandpa very busy," said the little girl in a Chinese accent as she appeared to be dumbfounded.

"Listen, little girl, run along to the back and tell Mao Zen Dong to bring his ass out here, please?" said Fisher as he gave the girl a hard look.

The little girl quickly retreated as she made her way to the cooking area behind the counter while on the verge of tears.

"That wasn't very nice, Luke," I said sternly.

"Oh, whatever, I've never liked children anyway," he said as he began to bite his finger nails.

"A few minutes later, the little girl returned with an old man so thin and fragile, that he looked as if he could be snapped in two.

"We serve food and drink. If you no want, then go," he said in a very thick Chinese accent.

"We just want to ask you a few questions," I said.

"What?" he asked defensively.

After thinking about it for several moments, he then said, "Okay, let's go. But you, stay here," he demanded as he waved an old and wrinkly pointer finger at Fisher.

"Hell no," said Fisher adamantly.

"I can handle this," I assured him as I made my way to the back of the restaurant.

The moment he shut the door that led to the storage area of the restaurant, I turned around to confront the man. However, as I did, I barely managed to see a katana that nearly sliced my neck off as I got out of dodge. The man then went back and forth in motion as he tried to slash me with his sword. I quickly avoided all of his attempts as I swiftly made my way into the kitchen and tried to find something to use for self-defense.

One by one, plates, cups, jars and everything in between smashed upon the ground as the old man quickly knocked them down like a batter waiting for a pitch. Before I knew it, he then ran up on me and attempted to bring the sword upon my throat as I grabbed his wrists with both of my hands. As we struggled with the sword, I kicked him in his shins twice before he stumbled and collapsed onto the stone hard floor. After doing so, the little girl entered the room and pulled out a chrome black .44 when I said, "Nuh-uh. You wouldn't want to lose your Grandpa here, would you?"

I then grabbed the sword and placed the root of its tip upon the flesh of his neck.

The Chinese man then spoke to his granddaughter.

"No," he said, followed by some other words in Chinese that I could not understand.

"Didn't I say I wanted this to be simple?" I asked as I fixed my hair while keeping a firm grasp upon his tiny little body.

"What you want with me?" he asked as he began to sputter due to the pressure of the katana upon his throat.

"Tell me a little about Mark Gambini," I told him.

"Please, I don't want any trouble," he begged.

"I'm not trying to cause any trouble sir, just please, tell me what you know," I said as I flashed him my BKPD badge.

"Okay, well, Mr. Gambini used to come here every Thursday night with his men. On Thursday, they come and eat plenty. Sometimes, they come in and boss me and my granddaughter Xao-Lin around," he said.

"Go on," I urged him.

"And so, one day he came in with a dead body."

"Just like that?" I asked.

"Yes. In plastic bag. They had just commit a murder and they ask me to help them put body in dumpster out back."

"So, what happened?" I asked.

"After they put body there, they have guys come to make pick up approximately four hours later around one in morning," he exclaimed in his thick Chinese accent.

"And then what?" I pressed on.

"Nothing. I don't see him for last whole month. But I'm scared that he will come back and eventually kill me," he said in a fearful voice. "When I saw you, I thought you work for him," he added.

27

"Do you know where I can find him?" I asked.

"Don't know for sure. But I heard him mention a club in East New York last time."

"Do you remember the name of the club?"

"No, I'm very sorry."

"It's okay, thanks for your help, sir," I said with a slight bow.

"No, thank *you!* I'm sorry if I cause you any trouble," he said, before returning my bowing gesture with his very own.

"It's okay, really," I assured him with a gentle smile.

As I made my way to the front of the restaurant, Fisher had been trying the bread appetizers at one of the restaurant's tables.

"Everything okay?" he asked as I approached him.

"Yeah," I said as I rubbed the back of my neck and massaged it carefully.

"What now?" he asked.

"Let's pick it up tomorrow," I said as we left the restaurant.

"Want a ride home?"

"Sure," I said as I looked up into the heavens.

As I glanced upward, I noticed that the blue sky had turned into a burgundy kind of color. It was only after carefully examining it that I saw the dark gray coating of the evening sky itself.

28

V

Later that evening, I found myself unclothed and kissing Luke Fisher profusely upon the bed of his Canarsie apartment...We had just finished committing an act that made me feel good, terrible and ashamed all at the same time.

"Shit, it's seven o'clock, I definitely have got to get going," I said as I hastily slapped my watch onto my wrist and adjusted the strap of my bra.

"Hey, what's the rush?" asked Luke flirtingly, as he kissed me on my neck and rubbed my chest in a way that made me shiver immensely.

"Luke, listen, we can't do this anymore...you know that I shouldn't be here," I said to him as my rotten sense of guilt began to seep in through my pores.

"Oh, c'mon Deb, tell me that you love him more than you love me. I want you to look me directly in the eye and say it," said Luke with a resounding tone of confidence.

"Luke, we've been through this. If we would have started talking just a bit sooner, we probably would have—"

And with that being said, I never finished the sentence as I swiftly arose from the bed and went into the bathroom to fix myself up.

When I returned to the bedroom fully dressed, all Luke could do was stare at me as I finished tying my hair in a ponytail.

"Besides," I said, as if I continued where I had last left off, "aren't you messing around with that Jennifer girl, anyway?"

"Yeah, but it's *you* that I want. And don't try to act as if you don't want me too."

There was no doubt that my feelings for Luke ran deep, but at the same time, Daniel and I were to be wed soon. Therefore, I had to end it. In no way did I desire to be an unfaithful wife.

"Lane," scoffed Luke, before continuing, "the both of you have the same last name. And how do you know that you aren't marrying your long lost brother or something?"

"I've told you already, my father is black, and *his* is white."

Luke said nothing as he grappled with the thought of us not being together.

"And Luke...this just can't happen anymore. This is the very last time. Believe me when I say it...I'll see you tomorrow before we head out to that club," I said as I buttoned up the collar of my maroon shirt.

And without another word, I left him alone in his apartment and caught the L train headed towards the city.

Hidden Pleasures: In truth, my romance with Luke had been heating up for quite some time, however, there was no more that I could possibly do. My heart belonged to one man and one man only, and as of that day, I made it my duty to never again find myself crossing those boundaries, or at least, I sincerely hoped that I wouldn't...

VI

The next morning I was very surprised to find Fisher at the office before me. It was a quarter to eight when I found him digging through file cabinets possibly searching for new documents on the case.

"Morning," I said to him as I removed the sweater that I had on and hanged it neatly upon the mantel piece.

Fisher steadied his gaze on the file cabinet as he replied with a simple grunt while he separated stapled documents.

My reaction to this sudden silent treatment was peaceful and neutral. It was obvious that Fisher was still flustered by the comments I had made the previous night. As hard as it had been for me as well, there was no way that I would have allowed him to unhinge me mentally and emotionally. Fisher had a job to do and so did I.

"Lane, report to the conference room now," said Captain Gordon after he had opened the door.

"Fisher, what are you doing here so early? Aren't you on patrol right about now?" asked Gordon as he checked his watch.

"Well sir, Lane asked me to—" he started.

"Just meet me in the conference room," I interrupted before he could finish.

And without another word or a glance, Fisher headed out of the office.

"What's going on?" asked Gordon as he studied me carefully.

"Fisher's with me on this one," I said as I gathered the remainder of files that Fisher had left upon the counter.

"And when were you going to tell me this?" he asked as he continued to study me.

"Today, as a matter of fact," I said.

"Are you sure about this? Fisher, I mean?" he asked uncertainly.

"Positive, cap," I replied with confidence.

"Okay, well, I'll meet you out there then," he said, as soon as I had walked past him.

After several minutes of chatter while waiting for protocol within the conference room, fraternization immediately ceased as Gordon appeared with files at hand. As he stood before us and observed all that were seated and present, he strongly cleared his throat.

Gordon was an attractive and firmly built white man in his early fifties. He had the physique of someone who had been in the Navy as he possessed thick, broad, and muscular shoulders. One would have never been able to guess that he was pushing 59 years of life due to his clean and shaven baby face.

Even after all of his years serving as the captain of the 23rd Precinct, there was no doubt that he looked incredibly young, despite his age.

"Gentlemen," he said after making sure that he had everyone's attention.

I then harshly cleared my throat to confirm my presence.

"And ladies," he said sheepishly before continuing.

"Today is the day where we seriously get the ball rolling. I know that yesterday I kind of gave you the entire background scoop as to what it is that we're precisely up against and now I am anxious to hear what exactly you guys have compiled since then."

"Well, apparently he's been stashing an import of cocaine from Colombia in warehouses throughout the city," said detective Travis Williams who wasted no time in reading information off of a worn, and yellow, notepad.

"How about you, Alvin?" asked Gordon.

"Nothing much on my end," he said, before adding, "each time that I've hit the streets to rap with the supposed informants; they've all claimed to lack sufficient information."

"We all know that's a goddamn lie," said Fisher as the rest of the room murmured in agreement.

"As Williams stated earlier, we know Gambini's crew has manufactured, shipped and smuggled drugs within various warehouses throughout Brooklyn. Word spreading around town is that for every shipment of furniture or clothing, he'd also package cocaine along with them before shipping," said detective Alvin.

"But if I'm not mistaken, I could have sworn that you said Gambini's sole priority is organized crime," added Williams.

"Yes, that is very true. He doesn't just import or export his goods. What he'll often do is have his men murder a crew that thinks he's on their side all along. After intercepting their product, he takes it all on from there."

"I've got something for you captain," I said as I suddenly broke my silence.

"Let's hear it," he replied as he rolled up the cuff links of his dress shirt.

"Yesterday evening, Fisher and I made a trip to Gambini's favorite Chinese buffet called Loon Hung and we found out that he and his men once smuggled a corpse into the back of the establishment."

"Really?" he asked.

"Yes and we also discovered that he and his men often spend time at East New York Club on Liberty Avenue."

"Well, I'll be damned, Lane. Please be sure to head out there tonight and as for the rest of you coppers, I would like for you all to contribute anything that you may find of value to Lane and Fisher as time pushes forward. Do I make myself clear? Alright, dismissed!" he commanded.

The entire conference room filed out one by one as Gordon caught me alone in the corridor of the west wing as I headed back to my office.

"Great job," he said, and then continued, "if you happen to need help, any help at all, be sure to let any of the other detectives know."

I nodded to show that I would if needed.

"When are you checking out Club Lounge exactly?" he asked.

"Tonight," I replied.

"If you need anything," he said reassuringly as he softly squeezed my shoulder.

"I'll manage," I told him, "really, I will."

And without another word, he quickly turned the corner as I was sure that he had returned to his office.

At four o'clock, I made sure to immediately wrap up what I had been doing in the office in order to head home for a brief rest. As I walked towards the train station, I happened to notice detective

Luke Fisher's Acura in the parking garage outside of the precinct.
I was glad that I hadn't bumped into him. I had promised that it
was the end and the last thing I needed was to take a detour while
on my way home…

VIII

Later that night, I met Fisher just on the outskirts of Liberty
Avenue upon the same block that the club was located.   As we
neared the entrance we saw a bouncer who resembled the likes of
an NFL linebacker. He was thick, black, muscular, and had a
shiny bald head that glistened in the streetlights. He had a hard
look about him that screamed, "*try me.*"

"I.D?" he said.

I swiftly drew out my badge and flashed it to him.

"We're here on official police business," I said.

"Who are you?" he asked.

"We're detectives Lane and Fisher of BKPD's 23rd precinct.

"The 23rd precinct?" he then asked in a serious tone.

"Yeah, why, what's up?" responded Fisher who looked past
the bouncer and peered into the club.

"Does the name Frank Matthews ring a bell?" said the
bouncer.

"He's our homicide detective specialist," I said.

The man simply chuckled before saying, "Take a look at my right ear."

The moment I decided to give it a look, I instantly regretted that I had. The bouncer had a good chunk of flesh missing straight down the middle of his right ear lobe. It looked as if a rabid wolverine had torn a piece off while making a conscious decision to let the bit that remained dangle in mangled fashion forever.

"Now, I'm not certain if it was him three years ago who did this, but if it was, you be sure to tell him where I'm working now and that he'll eventually get what's coming to him one of these days."

"Look, all we want to do is—" I protested.

"You're good, just don't cause any trouble in here tonight," he cut in as he let us pass without even another glance.

After entering the club, Fisher couldn't resist sharing his feelings upon what we had just witnessed.

"Did you see that shit? The man's ear looked like a knifed sausage," said Fisher as he shuddered.

"Yeah, I know," I said as we worked our way through the packed club of people dancing all over each other.

"If Matthews was the one who did such a thing, let me just say that he did one hell of a job," exclaimed Fisher in an amused voice.

We continued to walk around the club as we hoped to spot anyone that looked extremely suspicious or that could have helped with the whereabouts of Gambini and his men.

"If Gambini does come here, you know that he'd maintain a low profile. No way would he allow himself to be easily accessible," said Fisher.

"You're right, maybe we should ask the bartender over there," I said as I pointed to an Italian, broad shouldered man who was busy serving drinks at the bar.

The moment we approached the bar, the man simply looked at us with his glassy brown eyes and said, "What's it going to be for you two lovebirds?"

"We're not a couple," I assured him.

Luke Fisher rolled his eyes as he uncomfortably adjusted the brim to his ruffled hat. It was obvious that my stance on not acknowledging him as anything more than just a co-worker perturbed his nerves.

"Alright, well anyways, what will it be?" he asked with a jolly fat smile that resembled the likes of a kid on Christmas.

"We're with the BKPD," I said as I flashed him my badge.

"Po-police?" he asked dumbfounded.

"Yes, and we'd like to ask you a few questions," Fisher cut in.

"Oh, I'm sorry, but I really can't help you," he said as his voice suddenly became shaky.

"Actually, I think you can," I said as I concentrated on his face.

Beads of sweat began to pour down his forehead immediately, when he abruptly mumbled something about having to use the restroom.

"Just give me a sec, please," he said.

After fifteen minutes had passed we automatically realized that the bartender had played us for a fool.

"Deb," said Fisher as he went behind the bar and scoured its contents.

"Say no more," I said as I poured myself a drink. We've gotta go."

"Excuse me, can I get a shot of vodka? And also, a rum and a coke for my dear lady here," said a man who was thin and going bald.

He wore an open collared dress shirt with sleek, dark slacks. As for the woman that accompanied him, she wore a fiery red dress that displayed her curvaceous shape. She was a blonde who had very long hair and a smooth round face and her eyes were a clear ocean blue that resembled pacific water.

"I'm sorry, we aren't bartenders," said Fisher as he organized every wine, champagne, or beer bottle that his hands had come across.

"Seriously, Mark's gotta step it up around here," said the man. "C'mon, Edie, back to the dance floor we go."

And without a second's hesitation, they melted within the dance floor as the population of the club itself, dissolved them as they had come.

"Let's just call it a night, Luke," I said earnestly.

He quickly grabbed my hand and pulled me out of the club. As we headed towards his car, I noticed that we were still holding hands.

"Umm…Luke?" I said.

"Yes?" he asked, apparently engulfed deep within his thoughts.

And as he looked at me, one quick gaze at our hands told him everything that he needed to know.

"I'm sorry," he said as he suddenly released it.

He then went red as we continued to walk in silence without another word.

IX

Midnight came and went as we found ourselves cruising around the entire borough of Brooklyn. We had been all throughout town searching for anything that would give us a clue as to Gambini's whereabouts.

"Just drop me off at the nearest train station," I told him as I found myself utterly fatigued and done for the night.

"Sure thing," he said.

Fisher speedily turned down Nevins Street as his car came to a screeching halt a block away from the 2 train station. As he did so, it was then that we recognized the bartender from Club Lounge on Liberty Avenue exiting a CVS pharmacy with a shopper's bag in hand.

"Luke, look," I exclaimed as the bartender descended into the station.

"Is that—?" started Fisher.

"Let's go!" I replied.

Nothing else was said as we silently followed him into the subway. After buying metrocards, we feared to have lost him until we found our guy waiting on the 2 train platform headed uptown.

"How are we going to do this?" asked Fisher.

"I don't want him to run off again. So here's the plan. Walk all the way down the platform and get on one end of the train, while I'll be on the opposite end. That way, we'll be able to trap him if we have to."

Sounds like a plan," he whispered.

"Go, go, go!" I demanded in a stern manner.

As Luke and I departed, I knew that we would get some answers from the bartender. In no way was I going to allow him to slip through the cracks again.

After boarding the 2 train, I sat down just a short distance from him as I patiently waited to make a move.

The entire train ride he never left my sight until I finally decided to approach him at the Fulton street stop.

"Hi, again," I said as I advanced towards him.

After a few moments of mental recollection his face turned into a depressed frown as he dropped his head and stared at the floor.

"Next stop, we're going to have a brief talk," I said in a serious manner.

The moment the train had come to a complete stop at Park Place, he got up with a start as I began to escort him off of the train. However, as I attempted to radio dispatch Fisher, he immediately re-entered the train with the door half way through closing. I instantly reacted by narrowly entering the crack at top notch speed.

Once making it back on in one piece, he ran hurriedly through the compartment doors as the train started to move. I kept running after the man until I finally caught up to him by the third compartment. He then took one glance at me before proceeding to open the next car door when Fisher suddenly emerged from the other side and swiftly pinned him to the ground with a strong thud.

"Great job, Luke," I said as I caught up to the both of them.

"What's your name sir?" asked Fisher as he held a firm grip on him.

"Joe Pisano," he said in a muffled voice as Fisher had pinned his face upon the dirty floor of the train.

In that moment, every passenger aboard the car stopped what they had been doing to watch us interrogate Pisano.

"We only wanted to ask you a few questions last time. Why'd you run?" I asked.

"Because of him," said Joe as he struggled to pry Fisher off.

"Me?" asked Fisher in disbelief.

"No, not you, Mr. G." he said through tight lips as he tried his hardest to keep his face from making contact with the floor.

"Gambini, you mean?" I said.

"Yes. You see, he holds a lot of shares through investment of that club, so there ain't no telling what could have happened or what I would've said to you guys if I'd stayed there."

"How long has he owned his shares?" asked Fisher.

"Not that long to be completely honest. Maybe about three years or so."

"What's he doing? How exactly does he make the money to profit off of a place such as Club Lounge?" I asked.

"His imported transactions from Colombia," he replied.

"He's getting product from the island which he then ships out in a factory to dealers throughout the city."

"Know any of the dealers?" asked Fisher.

"Yeah, there's Mercer, Fletcher, Jackson, Carter, Wallace—"

"Forget the dealers, what's the location of the warehouse in which his shipments are located?" I demanded.

"It's called Big Apple Moving and Storage Inc. It's right off of Atlantic and Pacific."

"How do we know that you're telling us the truth and aren't leading us into a trap?" quizzed Fisher.

The man named Joe started to cry as he blew his nose into his sweaty and dank shirt.

"Look, I never meant to get involved in any of this, okay? One night at work they wanted me to bring up a long island to Mr. G and so one of his men overheard me by the door as I dropped a plate that was also in my hand at the time. After catching me, they threatened to physically injure and as well as kill me if I ever said a word about anything. And, since then, they've kept a very close eye on me."

"But why did you run out of the club tonight?" I said.

"Yeah, what was your reason for vanishing all of a sudden while leaving your post unattended? Was he there?" asked Fisher.

"I don't think so but he could have been. That entire establishment is under surveillance."

"Listen, do you think that you'll be able to testify for us in court once we apprehend him?"

"Umm, I just don't know," he said as he looked out of the moving train's window.

"It'll be alright," I tried to assure him.

"We'll even put you into witness protection. He won't be able to touch you," I added.

"Sure, whatever, I just really want my life back," he said as he choked back more of his tears while the train screeched as it advanced deeper into the city.

X

The next day Fisher and I had informed everyone within our unit about Gambini's moves.

"It makes perfect sense," said Gordon. "Using a popular warehouse where drugs wouldn't be expected in order to solicit them. One wouldn't think to check a place such as that."

"So what's our next move?" asked detective Williams.

"We infiltrate the warehouse," said Gordon in simplest terms.

"Today?" he asked.

"No, tonight," assured Gordon as he thought long and hard about a possible course of action.

"Now, I'm going to need all of you to be on deck tonight. We're going to surround the parameters of the warehouse in its entirety. That means it is mandatory that every single unit be there. You all should be dressed in full combat attire. We'll meet here tonight at six and we will supply you with everything that is needed for the task. Am I clear? Eighteen hundred hours! Nothing more, nothing less!"

And with that being said, the entire unit quickly departed and left the room empty.

As he was making his way back towards his office, Captain Gordon caught up to me and said, "It's your time now. Show us what you're made of."

After watching him turn the corner, an internal voice inside of my head said, "Yeah! It's time to *show* them what you're made of!"

XI

At a quarter to five we all reconvened at the precinct. We had a job to do and were prepared for whatever that would eventually occur. Stationed in the middle of the combat room were two large vaults that contained gear for the infiltration and also artillery for a more than likely showdown.

"How do I look?" asked Fisher as he clumsily placed a helmet upon his head.

"Charming," I said as I tried to resist a smirk.

"Ladies and gentleman. Are we ready?" asked Captain Gordon as he entered the room fully dressed and prepared.

There was no doubt that he was certainly ready for battle as his combat boots were laced all the way to the tip of his knees and his M-40 lied neatly upon his back with a silver shoulder strap to support it.

After surveying the room and seeing everyone waiting for the next command, Gordon then said, "Let's move out!"

XII

Captain Gordon made sure that the entire warehouse was surrounded upon arrival. He had the whole Third Avenue blocked off as well as both Atlantic and Pacific Avenues.

"Hey cap, you keep everything in order out here. I'm going to have a few of us infiltrate the interior while proceeding with caution," I said forcefully.

Gordon gave me a long hard look before saying "Just be careful."

Twenty minutes later, Fisher and I had ten men that were ready to penetrate the warehouse. It wasn't long after when we suddenly heard massive gun shots being exchanged on the other side of the building.

"Where do we start?" asked Fisher as we thought of different scenarios that would help us sneak into the warehouse.

After fifteen minutes of searching, another female detective from the precinct found a secret door that was hidden within the concrete.

After countless attempts at breaking in, Fisher then asked if any of us female detectives had hair pins. The same female detective that discovered the door gave him one on the spot as she immediately removed it from out of her hair which was tied up in a bun.

"Thanks, you've just been coming through for us today, haven't you?" said Fisher as he gently took the pin from her.

The woman who I was sure worked in the bomb squad unit lowered her head slightly as her face had flushed pink.

"Forget it, it's nothing," she said coolly after looking up and beaming at Fisher.

Look at her trying to be cute, I thought as my face turned red.

"Got it," said Fisher as he finished picking the lock.

"You're a pro, huh?" I said as I tried my hardest to get next to him.

"Well, when you spend five years on the streets you're bound to learn and retain some things," he said as he took the hair pin and tucked it deep inside of his pocket with a spry smile.

And from there, we quickly descended down the stairs as we made our way into the warehouse basement.

"Stick together, but move silent," I said as we worked our way down a tunnel with rifles and semi-automatics strapped onto our shoulders.

As we entered a dark corridor, the sounds from the gun battle waging in front of the warehouse increased with every step. The echoes of bullets going back and forth were accompanied by the falling of shattering glass. Somewhere above ground, the BKPD had obviously made it an agenda to strike every window, in order to have better chances of rapid open fire. And so, after what seemed like twenty minutes, the corridor finally came to an end.

"Okay, weapons ready," I said as I opened a door that led into the first level of the warehouse.

We then silently entered the room one by one when we saw a group of Italian men who were shooting with semi-automatics on the opposite side of the warehouse.

Fisher had pulled out his .44 when the other policemen began to draw their weapons as well.

"Hold your horses," I told them before they had a chance to do anything.

After looking around and seeing what was being presented at first glance, I immediately crafted a plan.

"Fisher, you take five of our men with you and set up post over there, you five, come with me," I said as I led them to a corner of the warehouse that gave us clear angles for fire.

From where we had positioned ourselves, the side angles of Gambini's men were exposed. They would soon have no idea as to what was going to hit them.

"Okay, you see those five men up top over there?" I asked as I pointed to several men with snipers keeping a constant eye out for intruders.

"If we don't hit them soon, eventually they are going to see us; therefore, they are the first set of guys that we have to eliminate. They've got AMR's, M40's and only God knows what. Fisher and his guys will do their best to take out all of the ones on the ground level. But as for us, we must take out all of the ones from up top, got it? Oh and please do your best to use the least amount of bullets that you possibly can. Just connect and keep moving, I want to have all of them guessing. After we work our way through them, we can cover for Fisher and the others. Alright guys, move, move!" I demanded.

I then showed my men that I meant business as I aimed my pistol and hit a gunman posted near a railing right in the chest.

After he collapsed onto the floor, I swiftly hit another gunman as he too, fell upon the ground. In a sudden state of panic, the armed men started firing rapidly in all directions. However, with great poise, my unit continued to aid me as we took them all out one by one.

When we were sure that we had gotten all of them, we then joined the shootout as bullet shells were seen scattered throughout the floor as the fire between both groups continued.

"We've put down the majority of them!" yelled Fisher behind the sounds of gunfire.

"Any sign of Gambini?" I asked.

"Nope, none whatsoever," he screamed as he reloaded his .44.

"We need to find him fast, he can't be far off," I yelled back.

"Oh of course, so what's the-?"

Luke, however, wasn't able to finish the sentence. A blast from an opposing gun made him fall back as he looked at me wide-eyed with fear.

A hole had been carved within his bullet proof vest as he suddenly started to gasp.

"NO!!! MAN DOWN!! Guys, please, HELP!!!" I screeched to my crew as I made my way over to him.

Not long after, seven of the 23rd precinct's policemen had made their way to where Fisher lied clutching his chest and breathing heavily.

"Deb, Deb," he said as he gripped his chest

"You're going to be alright," I promised him.

"Quick guys, put pressure on it. See if there's any wound."

"You," I said to the female cop who had smiled at Fisher earlier.

"Listen, I want you and three of you guys in general to get Fisher outside to a paramedic. Use the narrow entrance that we came in through. And as for you guys, I want you all to head out. We can't risk anyone else getting hurt. I'm going to exit out of that side door over there and see where it takes me."

"You got it," said Williams from beneath his helmet. "Move out fellas, move out," he added as they ducked and dodged the incoming fire of bullets from the remaining armed men.

I then rapidly jetted out of the warehouse side door when I saw the thin man from Club Lounge whose hair was balding, as he placed a heavy crate into the back of an armored truck. In the passenger seat was a guy who had the face of a mob boss. He had slick brown wavy hair, blue eyes and had on a pin-striped gray suit.

"Freeze!!!" I cried as I pulled out my .45.

"Drive," said the man in the passenger seat as the engine started.

The armored truck wasted no time as it then began progressing its way down the narrowed strip of Third Avenue.

I swiftly jumped into an abandoned patrol car and chased after them. As they weaved in and out of the Brooklyn city traffic, I immediately thought of something that would prove to be very risky.

And so, as they made their way down Tenth Avenue, I turned left onto Bergen.

After taking the left, I drove another three blocks up and turned right onto Tenth as I met them coming at me with full force.

I then ducked and tucked myself under the driver seat as I felt the impact of the truck hit and sent it spinning sideways before crashing into a traffic light pole. As I looked up and out into the street, all I saw was mayhem as a plethora of cars had been wrecked or completely totaled due to a sudden massive pile up.

After leaving the wreckage of the patrol car behind, I took notice to a nasty gash on my right forearm. The impact of the truck had sent shards of glass flying from every single direction as a big piece unmistakably cut me. Besides wincing a bit after making my way up and out of the vehicle, I barely felt any pain as I walked towards the totaled front of the getaway truck. As I peered inside, I saw that the driver was dead as his head lied upon the steering wheel covered in blood.

After carefully observing the man next to him, I suddenly realized that he was certainly who we had been searching for all along, none other than Mark Gambini.

Gambini bled profusely as he clutched his left arm. His eyes were closed shut while he made constant piercing groans.

It was then that a swarm of patrol cars pulled up and engulfed our presence. As I saw Captain Gordon approaching me, I took out my pair of handcuffs and cuffed the suspect.

"You have the right to remain silent when questioned. Anything you say or do may be used against you in a court of law. If you cannot afford an attorney, one will be appointed for you before any questioning, if you wish," I said.

Gambini looked up at me stupidly as he let out a final and heavily defeated moan.

"This calls for a celebration and some medical care," said Gordon in a pleased tone as he examined my shoulder.

"Detective Lane, you have shown a huge amount of bravery this evening. You are now granted exclusive access to any unit you choose to be a part of. I am also promoting Fisher as I now welcome him into the 23rd precinct's burglary/narcotics unit as a first rank detective. Congratulations to the both of you," he then said cheerfully.

"Oh my God, Fisher! How is he?" I said in a worried voice.

"He's alright," answered Gordon with a smile.

"The vest caught the bullet just before it could truly do any damage. As the paramedics carted him into the ambulance they said that in about two weeks' time, he should be as good as new and back to work. Luckily for us, it's nothing too serious. I mean, he was asking for grape juice and hot dogs for pete's sake," said Captain Gordon with yet another smile.

I then let out a sigh of relief as I leaned my back up against the truck.

"Just great work, all of you," declared the captain as he looked at all of his policemen on sight.

"Now, let's get this place cleared up!" he ordered.

"And as for you," he said to me before I could walk away to a nearby ambulance for treatment.

"It looks as if you've got yourself a partner," he said.

I smiled as I made my way into the ambulance. Within a matter of seconds, the ambulance was roaring into the night as I felt it pick up speed upon reaching the expressway. And with every moment that passed as I sat and experienced the ride, I couldn't help feel anything but happy. I really had come through for Gordon, Fisher, the borough of Brooklyn and every member of the 23rd precinct in a very big way. But more importantly, just like Daniel had believed the day that I had told him, I was happy more than anything to know that I had certainly come through for myself.

Episode 3:

"Brushed Before Crossfire"

I

Detective Luke Fisher had been trudging along the precinct's corridors when he let out a huge yawn. He was exhausted from partying the night before in the Williamsburg section of Brooklyn. As he walked the path of the hallway, he felt his temple throb. He had a massive hangover and honestly wished that he hadn't shown up for work. Realistically, however, he didn't have a choice.

Everyone within the 23rd precinct had realized or came to their senses upon Fisher being one of those cops that did things on his own time and at his own pace. Sometimes, however, he didn't do anything at all, but when the time called for it, he would somehow, someway, manage to luck his way through.

As he entered the burglary/narcotics unit conference room, he managed to stifle yet another yawn and sat next to detective Lane by the door's entrance in stealthy fashion.

"Long night, eh?" she asked with a smirk.

"Yeah, I guess you can say that," whispered Fisher as he tried to remove some crust from his eyes.

"A little rendezvous with Jen? She must've been the aggressor I'm guessing," said Lane as she did her best to suppress a snicker.

"Care to share what it is that you find funny over there?" asked Gordon as he looked directly to where the source of the giggles had come from.

After no one answered, Gordon began to inspect every face of his detectives before keying in on one individual in particular.

"So glad that you could join us, detective Fisher," he said as he skimmed through some files that were in his hands.

"Tell me something, when you woke up this morning, did you once stop to think about being at work the time you were scheduled to be here for or do you just clock in whenever you happen to feel like it?"

"I can explain cap, you see—"

"Now is not the time for that. The time we have now is all about this case. See me afterwards, I'd like for us to discuss some things in private," fired Gordon as he leered Fisher with ferocious intensity.

It was obvious that he wasn't the slightest bit happy with his detective.

Detective Fisher simply folded his hands as he continued to stare at Gordon. His cheeks had also become magenta due to embarrassment.

"As I was saying ladies and gents, the safe that holds in-game revenue at Yankee stadium has just been robbed. We're still not exactly sure who or what group of people were behind such a heinous act, but trust me, we'll definitely get to the bottom of it," he said in a voice that almost sounded like a promise.

"How does this pertain to Brooklyn specifically and the 23rd precinct?" asked detective Travis Williams.

"I am glad that you asked that Williams. You see, apparently this Yankee stadium robbery has a close connection to the bank hits that have been occurring all over Brooklyn. Whether it's Bank of America on Flatlands, TD Bank near Manhattan Beach, or Chase Bank in Bensonhurst, these criminals have tackled these banks on a periodic schedule. For some reason, they strike on Friday evenings after everyone such as the clerks and bank tellers have gone home. Now, what we have to do is prepare ourselves for the next hit and make sure we're there just before they execute their plan," said Gordon.

"So you want us to sit back and relax until they rob another bank?" asked Fisher.

Every other cop seemed to have murmured in agreement as they thought that for once, Fisher had actually made sense.

"Of course not, we have a two week plan in the making here…What we've been allowed to do is launder about fifteen million to Wells Fargo, as supposed bait for the suspects. Now, I know this sounds really farfetched but I've gotten word from the BKPD commissioner that this same very tactic has been tried overseas in the past and has worked."

"Interesting," said Williams.

"Now, there has been word that it has failed but we are going to give it a shot anyway. If we don't even attempt to put a stop to this, it's only a matter of time before innocent employees are present and get hurt," proclaimed Captain Gordon as he caressed his cleanly shaven face.

"Most of you here have a job to do regarding this plan and will most certainly without question play a part in it. The two detectives that I'm assigning primary responsibility for this case will be notified by me personally. Got it? Dismissed!" he concluded.

As usual, every officer started to file out of the conference room.

Detective Fisher began to follow suit as he then trekked back out into the hallway. He had wondered in what form or capacity that he would be involved with the case. Unlike the others, he hadn't received word on what tasks would be expected of him.

As he thought about it more in depth, he had reached the end of the hall where his office stood, when suddenly, a booming voice from behind, yelled out, "FISHER!"

Fisher immediately whipped himself around to see that Captain Gordon and detective Travis Williams had then appeared exactly in front of him.

"Yes, captain," said Fisher as his voice suddenly became strong and sharp.

"It looks like you and detective Williams have a case on your hands."

Detective Fisher looked at the man known as Travis Williams. He was a no nonsense kind of guy who liked to ask a lot of questions. He was a bit on the short side at five foot six but what he lacked in height, he surely made up for it with sheer skill and heart. Detective Williams possessed a round hard face that appeared as if it could protect him throughout Brownsville. He was a rotund shaped man that also had thick, stocky arms in mid-transformation like an aspiring bodybuilder. The most striking feature about his appearance however, was his long and thick brown nose that seemed as if it could bench press three chimpanzees simultaneously.

"Where does detective Lane play a part in this cap?" asked Fisher as he dreaded the captain's answer.

"Lane has been assigned to a special project due to her extraordinary work and capabilities as of late. Therefore, this one is all yours. Detective Williams is not as active now as he once was before, but he will assist you in piecing the puzzle together, nonetheless."

"Is this change permanent?" pressed Fisher as he tried to make his question sound as casual as possible.

"No, I'm just interested in seeing what you can possibly do with different detectives at the helm, that's all," said Captain Gordon simply.

"Sure," said Fisher as he swiftly made a move for his office.

"And Fisher, don't you go asking Lane for any kind of assistance with this case. She's got a lot on her plate at the moment. If I receive any word of her coming to your aid, you can say hello to street patrol. Do I make myself clear?" said Gordon in a serious voice that showed he meant business.

"Yes sir," replied Fisher as he did his best to keep his gaze on the captain.

"Williams, I'll leave it to you two then."

And without another word, Captain Gordon swiftly departed and turned at the end of the hallway as he headed towards his office which resided in the east wing.

"Now listen here boy. I don't like to do a lot of walking around here, alright? I'm in my mid-fifties now and I'm just about tired of all this cop drama bullshit. So do what you gotta do and bring some of your things into my office down the hall. I'll even set up a temporary cubby space for you," growled Williams.

And before Fisher could process what had just been said, Williams rapidly disappeared. As he was again left alone, Fisher couldn't help but think that Gordon wanted Williams to monitor his performance. He then proceeded to look at his watch before heading into his office and snatching up some of his most important things.

There was no Deborah Lane to save his butt this time. Over the next two weeks, he'd be working side by side with Travis Williams.

II

Later on that day, Fisher was just about done carrying a lot of his personal items into his temporary new office when Williams said, "What's the matter with you boy? You've been moving your shit in here like Uhaul."

"It's nothing," said Fisher. "I just like feeling at home that's all."

"Well, I hope you don't feel too at home because once this case is over, you can get the hell out of here."

"You mean, you don't think Gordon will separate me from detective Lane?"

"No, you damn fool!" said Williams as he extracted some files from an old, dusty crate.

"Gordon would just like to see your strong points when she isn't at the helm of a case, that's all. He wants to see how good you are."

Fisher scratched his chin as he turned on the guest stationed desktop computer that sat in front of him. He had never taken the time out to seriously think that Captain Gordon had assigned him the case for his own professional benefit.

As he continued to be deep in thought, Williams took it upon himself to drop a big binder that contained a case of files onto the computer desk.

Detective Fisher, who had been startled by the impact of the binder while lost in thought, jumped.

"What's this?" he asked as he opened it and began to scan through the contents of its pages.

"A portfolio. It contains addresses and aerial photos of every major bank in New York City's five boroughs," replied Williams.

"What's the reason for it?" asked Fisher stupidly.

At that moment, detective Williams took his own right hand and smacked himself hard upon the forehead with his stubby fingers in disbelief.

"Jesus Christ kid, it's basically our means to an end. These guys that are conducting licks all over town must either have a map or portfolio of every major bank within this goddamn city."

"Not just Brooklyn then?" asked Fisher curiously as he surveyed the binder's pages.

Detective Williams had then given Fisher a horrified look of exasperation.

"Honestly, were you paying any attention to the captain when he was speaking in there?"

"Actually I really—"

"I don't wanna hear your answer kid. Just stick close to me over the next two weeks and maybe Gordon will start taking you a bit more seriously."

"So, where to first?" asked Fisher as he continued to skim through the binder.

"Yankee Stadium, it's where they hit last, remember?" said Williams as he closed the binder and stuffed it back into the crate.

"The boogey down Bronx it is then," said Fisher.

Around three p.m. that afternoon, detective Fisher and Williams had made their way to the south of Bronx as they exited the 161st subway station.

As they walked towards the entrance of the stadium, they saw two male security guards in mini patrol cars that were driving around the facility.

"Excuse me, can we help you?" asked one of the men.

He had a 1970's mustache and a vintage mullet.

"We're a part of the BKPD, we were wondering if we could possibly get inside of the stadium to chat with its owner or someone who is well connected to the stadium's financial safe," said Williams as he looked around the entrance.

"The stadium as well as its locker room, training room, and offices are all closed. The world series against the Arizona Diamondbacks has been placed on hold for about a week due to ongoing investigation by the BXPD," said the other security guard in the patrol car passenger's seat.

He was very tall with long legs that seemed as if they had been sucked inside of the car. Like his fellow security guard, he appeared as if he had walked right out of the seventies as his afro sat neatly and square upon his thick, round head. If he hadn't been working as a security officer, his rightful location would have possibly been playing basketball somewhere in southern L.A.

"Listen, we just want some answers that's all," said Fisher as he placed both of his hands within his coat pockets.

Fall had arrived and the fact that it was late October, it brought strong gusting winds that rushed past their surroundings while licking their faces throughout the process.

"I don't mean to be rude but maybe this just isn't your place. Like my friend Johnson said, the BXPD are handling everything," said the white security guard.

"First of all, if BXPD were up-to-date as us, they would know that the people behind this robbery have also robbed a lot of the big banks in Brooklyn," said Williams as he surveyed both security guards closely.

The security guards then exchanged glances of shock and revelation to the news.

"We're sorry, we had no clue," said Johnson.

"And you, what's your name?" asked Fisher as he scribbled notes into a little black notepad.

"Tom Bird," he said.

"What about you?" he then asked the black man.

"Calvin Johnson," he responded.

"Do you two know anything about the robbery that took place last weekend?" asked Williams as he pulled out a pen and pad from deep within his trench coat pocket and began to scribble notes as they went along.

"Well, the only thing we know for certain is that it happened very late in the day. There was no game or anything going on at the time. The stadium was definitely closed," said Bird.

"I see. Have you guys heard anything regarding to the culprits as of late?" asked Williams.

"No, nothing at all. The only thing we can tell you is that the money which was stolen from us, was money that was accumulated throughout the MLB playoffs in terms of fan attendance, merchandising, and as well as food and such," added Johnson.

"Whoever did this had a lot of balls," said Fisher as he rubbed his chin.

"Well, thanks for all of your help," said Williams.

"And do us a favor," he added as he tucked away his notepad. "Try to keep this on the hush. As much as we respect BXPD, this is rightfully our case as well, I mean, due to the extensive history behind it and all."

"Will do," said Bird, "law enforcement is definitely an area that we try to stay the hell away from. I mean, I don't give a damn that I'm a stadium security guard. I just gotta pay the bills, you know what I mean?" he said.

IV

"Well, what did you think?" asked Fisher, half an hour later, on a train ride back to Brooklyn.

"I thought they were being straight up," said Williams as he studied his notepad while the train rocked back and forth.

"I'll tell you what though, we've certainly got some ground to cover over the next two weeks into however long this will all play out," he added.

"What do you mean?" asked Fisher.

"We still have to devise a plan to corner these guys at Wells Fargo," said Williams.

"I'll catch you later," he then said, before getting off at Hoyt street.

When detective Fisher exited the train at Nevins, he walked towards his car which was parked right next to a swap meet factory. As he drove back to Canarsie, all he could think about was how he would help in catching the suspected criminals.

V

The following Monday, Fisher walked into the precinct bright and early. As he turned the corner that led towards Williams' office, he glanced back when he heard detective Lane call him from down the hall.

"Psst, Luke!" she whispered.

"Hey Deb, what's up?"

"Get in here," she said.

"Why are you whispering?" asked Fisher, the moment he had stepped into the office.

"I don't want anyone to see us in close contact while you're on this case."

"Then what was your reason for calling?" asked Fisher as he looked at his now vacant station.

There was no doubt that he longed for the safety and comfort of his emptied cubby space.

"So, I was just doing some poking around and I found some information that will help you in regards to your case."

"Well?" asked Fisher anxiously.

He was most certainly on edge as he didn't want to get caught by anyone in the office, especially Gordon.

"First off, the head guy you may be looking for goes by the name of Zach Richards. A British man who's alma mater is Columbia University and who used to be an investment banker on Wall Street. Word on the street is that he recently worked with local drug dealers by supplying them with weight as a way to advance his profit. Every huge amount of revenue that he garners, he supplies that money to kingpin's around the city. And so, from there, he always receives a cut from the dealers he invests in."

"Wait, this isn't making any sense. So tell me, how does this pertain to my case and the inevitable task at hand?" asked Fisher in his most curious of voices.

"I was getting to that," she chuckled as she caught on to Fisher's slight bit of sarcasm.

"You see, there's this Russian guy whose brother is a felon and is always getting into trouble. His name is Demetri Cheknov and apparently a lot of the guys connected to the importation and distribution of the city's coke have been around and interacted with Richards on some kind of level. He told me that his brother happened to come across him on numerous occasions but the word eventually got out because the dealers couldn't keep their mouths shut regarding the entire situation."

"Oh, I see," said Fisher as he paid more attention to her than he had before.

"I'm only telling you this because I know that you've got a little less than two weeks now before you and Williams decide to put whatever plan that you guys have into action," said Lane in a very candid manner.

"And it truly means a lot Deb, seriously, it does. Thank you for all of your help."

Then without another word, Fisher turned his back on Lane and walked out of the office and headed down the hall. As he entered the office of detective Williams, he noticed that he had set up a table in the middle of the room with a big sheet of eight by ten drawing paper plastered upon it. Also present upon the table were various markers, rulers and tape.

"Look who it is?" said Williams sarcastically without even turning his back in order to face Fisher.

Williams stayed busy as he placed more objects upon the table that were sure to be of use.

"I guess we're going to be devising our game plan?" asked Fisher as he sat down in an old leather chair and observed everything upon the table.

"Yep, Gordon is supposed to be here any minute now," said Williams with duct tape in his mouth as he rapidly ripped a piece to fix his slightly tattered paper basket.

The door had then suddenly opened which led to both Fisher and Williams turning around.

"Gentleman, pleasure to see the both of you," said Gordon as he entered the office out of breath.

"I hope you two will excuse me," he added.

"Lane and I were discussing something that was very important. So what do you have?" he asked as he sat down looking curiously at the sheet.

"You, my dear captain are looking at the game plan of the burglary/narcotics unit," said Williams.

Detective Williams wasted no time in marking up the drawing paper at hand.

"Wells Fargo," he said, "located in Manhattan on Lexington Avenue and the address number is seven hundred and thirty-one."

As he said this, he wasted no time in conjuring a visual of the bank and what it looked like from the outside.

He then placed a second eight by ten drawing sheet that was sitting inside of a cardboard box upon the table as he labeled the exact landmarks and sections within the bank.

"Me and Fisher have conjured a plan that consists upon the bank robbers getting into the bank and working their way towards the safe."

"Where does it go from there?" asked Gordon curiously as he tried to smooth out his ruffled hair.

"We let them think that there's a means of escape by allowing them to leave free of any hassles," said Williams.

"And then what?"

"This is where our other units of the 23rd precinct come into play. You see, I say we surround the entire premises and make sure that we have the entire establishment covered. But, by no means do we enter or shoot up the place unless they decide that they do not wish to comply with our demands peacefully. I say we try our best to keep this as clean and free of bloodshed as possible," said detective Williams as he rolled up both pieces of

8 x 10 drawing paper and had secured them neatly in cylinders with elastic rubber bands.

"Anything else on that?" asked Gordon.

"The bank has been kind enough to wire in twelve million dollars in counterfeit money that they will then place within the bank's safe next Thursday night," said Williams.

"Very good, just excellent," exclaimed Gordon in a jubilant manner.

"How about you, Fisher? What have you contributed to this, if anything at all?"

In that moment, Fisher pulled out the files that detective Lane had handed him earlier and confidently began to speak.

"We've got a name that's possibly mixed up in all of this. His name is Zach Richards. He used to be an investment banker on Wall Street. The word going around town is that he's very well in tuned with the city's federal shares and may have something to do with the city's recent bank heists. And as mentioned earlier, Williams hinted a lot of stuff that referred to them and bank robbers in the plural form. Well, the word on the street about this guy is that he's investing a great share of the money into the drugs that are permeating the streets. He's cashing in on all of the dealers and may be using some of their good men to hit up these banks."

Gordon looked at Fisher curiously for a long moment before saying, "Wow, I'm impressed Fisher. Keep up the great work. You see? I know you have it in you. It's just a matter of intensity and focus. Well, keep me posted gentlemen, I'll be sure to have a chat with the two of you later."

For once, Captain Gordon seemed to have departed from Fisher in a great mood. When he finally left and the two detectives were all alone, Williams said, "Ms. Lane never ceases to amaze me."

"What do you mean?" asked Fisher as he tried to play dumb.

"C'mon boy, I've been a senior grand larceny detective for twenty-five years, you don't think I'm stupid do you?" he asked with a smirk.

"Okay, yeah, it's true, I got help. But I didn't ask, I swear. I was headed here this morning when she called me into her office and gave me the tip," he confessed with his head down.

Detective Williams had unfastened the first two buttons of his collared shirt, when he made his way over to his desk and turned on his computer. He then sat down and perched both of his short stubby feet onto the helm of the desk.

"Lane mentioned it just before you walked in and told me not to tell you. I have a feeling that she wanted you to be well informed once Gordon came in," he said as he softly wrapped his knuckles upon the table.

For some reason detective Fisher couldn't find the voice to speak. Instead, he seemed to be more interested with a fly that was zooming across the office window sill.

"You know, I have the feeling that detective Lane really likes you," said Williams with a grin.

"Yeah, me too," said Fisher in barely an audible whisper as he stepped outside of the office in order to gain some fresh air.

VI

The following days that succeeded the meeting came and went as every detective contributed to the plans of the heist intervention. Many detectives were seen entering the office of both detective Williams and Fisher like clockwork. There was no doubt that the planned intervention was shaping up to be one of the biggest Brooklyn Police Department takedowns in years. Even Fisher seemed a bit more serious and focused than usual as he gave his undivided attention to everything that was going on around him. He knew that the stakes for the case was at an all-time high and he most certainly wanted to play a huge part in it.

On the afternoon before the heist, Captain Gordon met with all of the burglary/narcotics detectives inside of the conference room to discuss what the following evening would entail.

"Ladies, gents," he said briefly before taking a black marker and scribbling upon the wall's board.

After moving away from what he had just written upon the board a few seconds earlier, it was easy for everyone to make out the word, "BIG!!!" in capital letters.

"Tomorrow, this is what it's all about. Everything you do in there is big! Every single move you make is big," preached

Captain Gordon as if he was prepping up a championship caliber team for a Super Bowl showdown.

"And so, just remember the blueprint that we have laid out for you guys. Be sure to trust your gut, trust your instincts and mark my words when I say that by the grace of God, we'll catch these criminals."

Captain Gordon had went from coaching to preaching all in one sitting but nonetheless, his words of encouragement had fueled every officer that sat within the room.

"If there are any concerns in terms of what is expected of you all, be sure to speak directly to both detectives Fisher or Williams as I've mentioned before. The last thing I'll say and I've said it already is to *trust* your instincts. It's one thing to be focused, it's another to be prepared, but as you all may know, things have a way of not going according to plan. Lastly, any questions?! Great, dismissed!"

In usual fashion, the conference room started to murmur as each detective left one by one and headed home to prepare for what lied ahead. Captain Gordon had then made his way through the crowd and caught up with Fisher as well as Williams just before they too, could disperse.

"This is it fellas," he said.

"Yep," replied Fisher.

Williams nodded his head to Gordon with both of his hands resting inside of his pockets to express agreement.

"Tomorrow, we leave at four, regular time and then we reconvene at sixteen hundred sharp by the warehouse that I told you two about."

"Got it cap. No problem," said Williams as he unhooked his tie.

VII

Later that night, Fisher had just left KFC where he had ordered two buckets of crispy chicken when his Nextel dispatcher suddenly went off.

"Awww jeez, what does captain want now?" he said as he approached his car and sat his bucket of chicken upon the rooftop.

When Fisher had finally pried his phone from within the depths of his left jacket pocket, he saw that the identification screen read: *dispatch-20011019 Lane.*

Detective Fisher wasted no time in pressing the push-to-talk button.

"Go!" he urged.

"Luke, get your ass down to Wells Fargo on Lexington pronto," she said.

"What's up?" he asked curiously.

"You can't be serious, Luke! The bank robbers! They've just infiltrated the building through the back entrance."

"Wait, what? Are you sure Deb, how do you know for certain that—"

"GET DOWN HERE!" she bellowed over the dispatch speaker.

Luke swiftly revved up his car engine and sped towards the Manhattan Bridge. He couldn't believe what he had just heard. He then placed his hand in the back seat of his car in order to grab a piece of his KFC meal. After a few seconds of grasping at nothing but thin air, he suddenly realized where he had placed his food.

"Shit, my chicken!" he yelled in frustration as he pressed his foot hard on the gas pedal.

VIII

Less than an hour later after very bad city traffic, Fisher arrived at Well Fargo's where the 23rd precinct's burglary/narcotics division was standing outside of the establishment.

"Fisher, glad you could make it out. We were waiting for you," said Gordon as he clutched some notes that were handed to him by detective Lane.

"I'm sorry sir, you see, the traffic—"

"No need for an explanation, I need you guys to put your plan into action before those criminals attempt to escape," he said.

"There aren't any employees in there, right cap?" asked Fisher.

"The place has been vacant for the past two weeks, Christ, haven't you been listening?" said Gordon as he shook his head in bewildered fashion.

"We haven't got the time for this. Look, Fisher and I will lead some of the men inside. Captain, you just have the rest of the vicinity surrounded," said Williams as he pulled out a .45 and inserted a clip into it.

"Alright, let's move out," commanded Gordon as the rest of the police withdrew their weapons and followed the two detectives. As they did, more police cars pulled up as the BXPD, SIPD, QPD, and NYCPD gathered around the scene. Apparently every single police department in the city had seen it fit to put a stop to the madness that evening.

As they approached the screened glass doors, detective Fisher happened to look at Williams who obviously knew what he meant and nodded his head in approval.

Six shots suddenly rang out as Fisher fired his gun into the door, shattering it and sending shards of glass flying throughout the process.

"Go, go, go," yelled Williams as they all rapidly entered the bank.

Detective Fisher scanned amongst his fellow cops but couldn't find her. It was obvious that this time, he would have to go at it alone.

"Look, let's split up," said Fisher.

"Good idea," said Williams, "I'll take these ten and you go on and take the others. If you need us, don't hesitate to page for back up," he added.

"You got it," said Fisher as he signaled for the other cops to follow him.

As Fisher and his men patrolled and searched the last four floors, they didn't detect a peep from the bank robbers. In what felt like an hour of just constant back and forth between floor levels, Fisher noticed that it was starting to get dark.

"Those of you that have flashlights, take them out now," he whispered as he pulled out his own.

The more they evaluated the building, there was something that Fisher just couldn't understand. If the bank had been tightly surrounded and packed with detectives, how on earth then would the robbers have any means or chances of escape?

As he was deeply entrenched in thought, a gang of footsteps were then heard from a staircase not too far ahead from where they all stood. As he and his men withdrew their pistols, they noticed that the flashlights staring back at them were none other than Williams and his own men.

"Nothing," he said as the rest of his men surfaced one by one from out the staircase.

"This just doesn't add up," said Fisher as he scratched his beard. "The entire place is surrounded, the streets are completely barricaded and blocked off. They can't escape by any means of the neighboring buildings, because damn near every cop in the whole freakin' city is patrolling them. So with that being said, where in hell could they have possibly gone?" he asked.

"Maybe we should check out the base—"said Williams but in that same moment, the cops began to hear subtle movement from the ceiling above.

"Fisher, this floor is the last floor, right?" he asked as he looked up.

"Yeah, the only thing that could be up there is…"

"The safe room," they both chorused.

"Quick, you guys go up through the east end, me and my guys will take the west," said Williams.

As Fisher and his men reached the final floor which was very narrow and cramped, they noticed a silver steel door that had been secured by a combination code.

"BKPD as well as every single department in the goddamn city is here! You have nowhere else to run. Come out with your hands up!"

As Fisher concluded his sentence, rapid gunfire began to erupt as two of Fisher's men had been taken out.

"Take cover," he screamed.

But as he looked around, there wasn't any cover to take as the gunfire had come from the tiny vents from within the floor's ceiling.

"Shoot up," he screeched, "UP!"

Every cop began to follow orders as a massive gun firing occurred.

"Wait, stop, stop, STOP!" cried Fisher.

He then walked up as he pressed his ear upon the door and listened intently. The more he listened, he faintly began to hear the sound of a helicopter hovering from up above.

"Looks like they have a means of escape, alright," said another cop.

"There was a tiny window towards the left end of the safe room that Fisher had suddenly noticed.

As he ran towards it to look out of the battered window, he faintly saw what happened to be eight large duffle bags being thrust into a chopper as the sky completely became draped in darkness.

"No! Quick, someone help me bust open this door!"

They all kicked and nudged the door hard before suddenly realizing that it was useless.

"Doesn't anyone know the code?" asked a detective.

"It's right here! Move!" said Williams as he gripped a sledgehammer carefully with both of his hands.

"Where'd you find that?" asked Fisher in amazement as he gazed at the bronze hammer that was now being firmly grasped by his partner.

"Basement," said Williams after finally breaking apart the coded lock on his tenth attempt.

As they entered the room, they looked at the safe that was positioned directly in front of them. It was opened wide with nothing but solid, steel glistening metal as if it had just received a polished shoe shine.

"Now what?" asked Fisher.

"You see that ladder just over there?" asked Williams.

Fisher turned his head until he saw a wooden ladder perched near the top of the room's glass window.

"It leads to the roof, let's go!" he added.

As Fisher proceeded to climb, he heard sounds of the chopper taking off. And as quickly as he could, he crawled out onto the roof top of the building, until he found himself able to stand.

The chopper was now hovering sixty feet above ground.

Williams had just caught up to Fisher with his gun pointed directly at the chopper as he hesitated for a moment before reluctantly putting it down.

They weren't alone, however, as the twenty fellow cops within their unit had all made their way onto the roof top as well.

For a time, he studied the young detective's face until finally picking up on exactly what his young partner was thinking.

"That's just the nature of the game kiddo. You win some and you lose some."

Fisher continued to stare into space and couldn't help but think on how Williams' words were true. However, he couldn't deny the fact that if he had been more aggressive from the jump, the outcome of the case would have been much different.

They then continued to watch the helicopter glide within the glimmer of the distance until it eventually disappeared and was swallowed whole by the night's black sky.

Episode 4:

"Crying Wolf"

It was a very frigid day in the month of February, Valentine's Day to be exact. The year was 2002 and a cop from the BKPD's 23rd precinct was now off the clock and cuddled up upon a sofa within a Canarsie condo on East 85th with his girlfriend.

"We had a great time tonight, didn't we sweetheart?" asked the man.

"Of course we did. If you count falling on your ass about twenty times romantic," she said as she burst out laughing.

"Oh, shut up, Jen," said the man as he leaned over her to grab the remote that was dangling upon the edge of the sofa.

"Seriously, though. You were God awful out there, Luke. I won't put you through anything like that again, I promise," she said as she gently rubbed his chest.

"Of course not, because next time I'm picking the spot," said Luke as he opened up a bag of M&M's that were resting upon the glass table.

"Oh whatever," she said as she rose up from the comfort of her cop boyfriend to wash her hands.

She then proceeded to the kitchen cabinet as she grabbed two clean sparkling glasses as well as a fine bottle of wine.

As she poured the drinks into their glasses, Luke Fisher quickly shut the television as the eleven o'clock news came on.

"To us, and the last five years we've spent together," she said as they clanked glasses and started to drink.

After finishing their drinks, Luke placed both of their glasses upon the table as he advanced upon his fiancé.

"There's no other place I'd rather be right now," he said as he gently brushed his lips upon hers.

Before they knew it, Luke and Jen had begun to passionately kiss before the sudden ring of the doorbell broke them apart.

"Who the hell could that possibly be at this time?" asked Luke as he stared at the door and then at his watch.

"Maybe Captain Gordon is stopping by to wish us a happy five years on Valentine's Day," she said in a joking manner.

"If Gordon wasn't miserably married, I'd probably believe you. Besides, he's got me on dispatch. If he ever wanted to ruin my night with an abrupt case, that's the way he'd do it," said Luke before advancing towards the door.

"Who is it?" he asked before answering a set of knocks that could have woken up the entire building.

Luke's question was immediately answered the moment he had opened the door. Standing before him with close resemblance was Jake Fisher, Luke's little brother who was about two years his junior.

"Hey, big bro," he said before entering the apartment.

Jake Fisher was just as tall, mildly built and possessed a sharp eye like his older brother. His hair was cut so low that he could have been mistaken for bald if it had not been for the immense lighting within the apartment that gave distinction to his tiny hair follicles.

"What are you doing here?" asked Luke in a serious tone.

"C'mon, Luke. Is this any way to treat your younger brother? I'm home man," said Jake as if he was trying to make peace.

"Luke, you never told me that you had a brother," said Jen as she advanced towards where the two brothers stood.

"That's because I don't," he said as he looked at his brother in disgust.

"Why, hello there. I'm Jacob Fisher, but you can just call me Jake," he said as he put out a hand to shake.

"I'm Jennifer Ramirez," she said as she shook his hand with a smile.

"Sweetheart, go into the bedroom," said Luke as he didn't once remove his gaze upon his younger brother.

"I was just trying to be pleasant and—"

"NOW!" he demanded.

As quick as he had said it, Jennifer swiftly made her way into the bedroom door.

"Now, I may have been locked up for a minute, but that's no way to talk to a lady," said Jake with a smirk.

"Don't you ever tell me exactly how to talk to my woman, you understand?" said Luke menacingly.

"Look, I'm not here to cause any trouble or bust any balls. I'm just trying to get back on my feet, that's all."

"When did you get out?" asked Luke.

"About two weeks ago," replied Jake.

"Well isn't that nice. I guess you're trying to re-establish yourself in the drug game."

"Man, I've got bigger fish to fry. I'm like you big bro. I'm pretty much past that phase of my life. I just want to move on and start from scratch."

"Why should I believe you?" asked Luke cautiously.

"Shit, you ain't gotta believe it big brother. Just give me a chance and watch me grow," pleaded Jake.

"Man, we haven't spoken in almost nine years and now all of a sudden you think you can just come knocking upon my door?" asked Luke.

"You should be happy that I didn't hold anything against you. Not once did you come see me," said Jake as he stared at his brother with weary eyes.

"Right, a BKPD detective talking to his felon convicted brother in the pen about what? Narcotics and sports? Please, let's cut all of the bullshit, okay?"

"Listen. I'm past that, alright?" Everything. All of that is behind me. I just need a place to stay," he said peacefully.

"Well, I hope you have a good search in finding a place that suits you," said Luke coldly.

"Why can't I stay here?" he asked.

"Because you're *you!*" bellowed Luke.

"Oh, so what am I? A monster now?" asked Jake in a voice filled with rising intensity.

"Look…this isn't 1992. I'm not running around with you anymore. Those days are long gone," said Luke.

"Negro, did I even mention 92'? I didn't say not a goddamn thing about our troubled pasts. I came here for a chance to reconcile with my brother, start my post-prison life on the right foot and live out the rest of my natural-born existence in nothing but peace," said Jake.

"You're still here?" asked Luke annoyed.

For a moment, both men cross examined each other as if they were x-raying the other's internal organs.

"I know when I'm not wanted. But let me tell you something Luke. Even after all of these years, you still continue to look out for no one but yourself. I thought that you might've grown up since the last time we met, but you just haven't changed a bit."

And without another word, Jake left as Luke slammed the door shut right behind him. For a minute or two, Luke continued to stand at the spot where he had just finishing conversing with Jake. He wanted to believe that his little brother had gone straight but thought it was best to have Jake prove him wrong.

As Luke continued to contemplate his thoughts concerning his little brother, he unfortunately didn't have to wait long before he was given an answer.

Episode 5:

"Mercy for Murder"

Intro: *If you're reading this, let me just say that it's my turn to speak. Some of you may have heard of me, while a lot of you have not. Therefore, allow me to re-introduce myself. I go by the name of Alvin Alvin. Yes, you've read right. This is not a typo. I'm now a detective with seniority at Parkside Avenue's 23rd precinct.*

With over a decade's worth of experience, it often baffles me in terms of why I still work primarily with detective Matthews within the homicide unit. I mean, let's be honest here, simply put, the man is crazy! I don't mean your average Joe Schmo ordinary type of crazy either. I mean, sociopath, psychotic and schizophrenic kind of insanity. Forget 1993, there's gotta be something rooted deep within himself that has played a prolific role in terms of the man that you see before you today. Well, hopefully after my narration I'll be given a sense of clarity to where you and I, can possibly figure it out together. Follow along as I take you inside the world of detective Frank Matthews.

In these following pages, you'll find out what really happened before the crossfires at Columbus. I hope you're ready, it's going to get a little messy.

I

It just so happened to be one of those late nights when detective Frank Matthews had decided that he would go for a drink at the Trash Bar. He had pulled up in front of the establishment around one in the morning before finally making his way inside.

And to his luck, a seat just so happened to become available when he suddenly plopped himself onto a bar stool and waited.

After several minutes of being hounded and harassed by the other customers, Tim Norton, the bartender, finally made his way over to Matthews who was seated in the shadows.

"Well if it isn't my main man Frankie," he said in a jubilant tone.

"Hey ya, Timmy," replied Matthews in a low but clear grumble.

"What will it be?" he asked as he quickly picked up a glass from behind the bar.

"Just a beer. A Budweiser would be fine."

"Sure thing," said Tim obviously taken aback.

Tim Norton was a chubby little Irish man that resembled a leprechaun. His nose was pointy and long as if it was once a sharp pencil. His arms were short and plump due to the layers of fat that comprised the majority of his body.

As swiftly as he could, Tim waddled his little fat self to the counter in order to hand Matthews his drink.

"There you go Frankie, enjoy," he said as his crinkling smile forced his eyes to show off their layers of fat as well.

"Thanks Timmy," said Matthews.

"To be honest, I'm kinda surprised that you didn't order your usual long island," said Tim as he watched Matthews chug down his beer.

Matthews' eyes remained focus on Tim as he finished his entire bottle. Once he was done drinking, he sat his container down and let out an unmistaken loud belch. He then wiped his mouth before saying, "Ehhh, I don't know, I just wanted a beer tonight."

"Interesting," said Tim.

"Yeah," replied Matthews.

"How's work been treating you?" asked Tim as he leaned over the counter. "Anything funny as of late?" he added.

"Stupid shit, just different days," answered Matthews as he shook his head after letting out another repulsive belch.

"I understand. Just be careful out there Frankie, I worry about you sometimes, you know?"

"Don't fret Timmy, I haven't slipped up once. I've got everything under control."

They both had given each other a reassuring look when Matthews' Nextel dispatch suddenly went off.

"It better not be who I think it is," said Matthews as he dug within his inner coat pocket in order to retrieve the blaring phone.

"Shit, it's him!" he said.

"Gordon, huh?" asked Tim rhetorically as he removed Matthews' empty beer bottle from the counter.

"Sex with this guy must be terrible, honestly," he said as he debated on whether he would pick up the phone or not.

Tim then let out his signature burst of laughter.

"Oh brother," he said as he moved on to yet another customer at the end of the bar.

"Yes," said Matthews after he had picked up the dispatch.

"Were you asleep?" asked the captain.

"No," he replied.

Matthews had gotten to a point in his career where he felt as if the end was near and so he tried to keep his answers to Gordon as short as he could possibly make them.

"Well, listen up then," said Gordon after being assured that he hadn't caused a disturbance.

He then continued, "I've got a new assignment for you. This one right here is big. There's a lot that I have to tell you in regards to the case but I'll wait until Monday morning to inform. Now, detective Alvin has already been notified, but like I said, I'll go more in depth at the top of the week. Any questions?"

"None," said Matthews with a blank expression on his face as he held the dispatcher in place.

"Okay then, bye," said Gordon.

Matthews responded by making a noise that was half in between a snort and a grunt before ending the call on his Nextel dispatch.

"Christ," he said as Tim had returned to the edge of the bar.

"What now?" he asked as he patted his sweaty forehead with a small white rag.

"Another case, Timmy. I honestly think Gordon loves his work more than he does his wife."

Tim covered his mouth as he tried to suppress yet another chuckle.

The introvert and the bartender. *As he did this, Matthews slightly grinned all the same. Although he would have never admitted it, one could have safely said that Matthews truly enjoyed Tim's company. Tim had been the only person that Matthews remotely enjoyed being around over the past ten years.*

And so, after having another drink of Budweiser, Matthews had then decided to call it a night.

II

On Monday morning, detective Matthews arrived at the 23rd precinct and walked into our office within the homicide department.

"Alvin," he said to me after he had walked in and settled within his cubicle.

"Matthews," I responded as I removed bunches of paper that sat cluttered on top of our printing machine.

"What's the word?" he asked as he ate a candy bar and logged onto his computer.

"Gordon wants you to meet him in his office to discuss the ramifications of the new case."

"This shit never gets old," said Matthews as he rose up off of his chair and left our office.

As he walked down the hallway that led to Captain Gordon's office, Matthews decided to head towards the burglary/narcotics department instead. Matthews had known Gordon well enough to know that he wasn't in his room.

The moment Matthews had reached the office of detective Lane, he strongly wrapped his knuckles upon the office front door.

"Come in," said Gordon's voice from within.

As Matthews entered the space, he found Gordon as well as both detectives Lane and Fisher surrounding the office table.

"You called for me James?" he asked.

"Yes," replied Gordon hastily, "I need you and detective Alvin out searching for this guy."

It was then that Captain Gordon had reached into a folder and handed old photo documents and newspaper clippings to detective Matthews.

"His name is Ron Mercer. You'll be able to find him in the Bedford-Stuyvesant area of Brooklyn."

"Apparently, he's plotting a murder on a former dealer who snitched on one of his employees a few years back. I need the two of you out tracking this guy down ASAP!"

"Not a problem," said Matthews in a low but audibly clear grumble.

After tucking the newspaper clippings safely inside one of his inner jacket pockets, detective Matthews left the burglary unit without another word.

As he headed towards the office, he couldn't help but smirk when he looked at the photos Gordon had handed to him. The pictures were mug shots of a younger Ron Mercer during the late 1970's to early 1980's.

Once back inside our office, detective Matthews noticed that I hadn't been around and decided to make copies of Ron Mercer's photos with the copy machine. He then took the originals and folded them before placing them into his pants pocket.

Several moments later, I opened the door and walked in with a cup of coffee firmly sealed within my left hand.

"It's a little chilly out there," I said as I threw off my jacket and placed it neatly upon the back of my chair.

"Uh-huh," said Matthews as he stared at the computer screen.

"Oh," he added, before placing the copied photos of Ron Mercer onto my table.

"James gave me those. I'm not going to waste my breath explaining crap to you because he told me that you've already been informed."

"Yes, I have," I said while taking a light sip of my coffee.

"Alright then, I'm going on break at noon. I need time to figure this all out," said Matthews.

"Don't worry about a thing Frank, by the time you get back, I'll be sure to compile a full list of suspects to add onto anything you manage to find," I said.

"You know me too well by now kid. I guess this having a partner thing isn't so bad after all," said Matthews as he disabled the virus protection on his computer and muted its sound while he watched porn.

By noon, Matthews had stepped out for his lunch break when he decided that he would go pay Ron Mercer a visit. He hadn't seen him in quite some time but had received word that Mercer had relocated to another part of town. Red Hook, Brooklyn, to be exact.

About half an hour later, he arrived at the Red Hook Houses East complex and parked his 1982 Honda Accord adjacent to where the building stood.

Upon reaching the tenth floor, he knocked on the apartment door labeled 1019A.

"Who is it?" said an unfamiliar voice from within.

"Big Matt," replied Matthews as he waited for the door to open.

"Negro, who?" said the voice again.

Matthews was starting to get irritated.

"Just open the damn door," he then said sharply.

After about another ten seconds or so, the door opened slowly when a black male who looked as if he was in his early twenties stood before it.

"Come in," he said.

As he let Matthews walk past him, he then took out a .9 millimeter and placed it upon the back of his head.

"Now, don't move," he said.

"Does it look like I'm moving?" said Matthews as he yawned in boredom.

"I said shut up nigga and don't move! You got any heat on you?" he asked as he made a move for Matthews' pocket.

It had happened so suddenly that the gunman didn't even see it coming.

Without a second's hesitation, Matthews' elbow swiftly connected with the jaw of the stick-up kid. He then maneuvered behind him and slammed him to the floor as if he was a prime time professional wrestler.

"Please, don't shoot," sobbed the kid.

His mouth was now bleeding profusely as blood began to seep onto his shirt.

"Where's Mercer?" asked Matthews calmly as he had drawn his own gun and placed it under the boy's chin.

"He's in the room," said the kid as he continued to whimper upon the ground like a puppy.

"Big Matt!" said Mercer as he came into view accompanied by another young man wielding a gun.

"Put that down Clay," he said as he observed Matthews.

"Shit, it's been so long," he now said.

Matthews had finally removed his gun from under the chin of the stick-up kid that he had pinned to the ground.

"Nice to see you too," he said as he carefully placed his .38 back within the crotch of his pants.

"I'm so sorry about this Matt," said Mercer.

"It's cool. Do you have a minute?" asked Matthews.

"For you, I have a lifetime," he said as he motioned for Matthews to follow him.

"Aww, shut your cryin," said Mercer without the slightest hint of sympathy as he stared at the stick-up kid who remained whimpering upon the stone hard floor.

"Clay, get over there and help Gee up off the floor. And clean him up too."

The young man named Clay did as he was told as he and Gee both made their way into the bathroom.

"Big Matt," said Mercer with energy once he had closed the door that had led into his cramped room.

The room was a large and dirty one that seriously needed a renovation. Tarp was peeling from the walls and the floorboard itself was loose and a dirty brown color.

The floor squealed and cried with every step as Matthews and Mercer walked towards a vacant table.

"What made you come all the way out here to Hooverville?" asked Matthews as he sat on one of Mercer's oh-too-familiar wobbly-wooden chairs.

"It's real hot for me right now Matt. And so, I lay low. I don't want to get caught up in any of the foolish politics happening around the borough of Brooklyn," he said as he sealed up some hard white within a ziplock bag.

"Understandable. So those are your new guys out there, huh?" asked Matthews.

"Yeah man, they've only been employed for about five months now. The last pair of guys I had wanted to back out of the game completely and so I had to get rid of them. But anyway, what's up?"

"You are," replied Matthews as he handed him the newspaper clippings and original photo documents that Gordon had given him.

"Damn! Oh my, yes these are nice," said Mercer as he observed his mug-shots before carefully thumbtacking them upon his wall as if he had been inducted into a hall of fame.

"I sure as hell was the looker back in my day, huh?" he now said more to himself than he had to Matthews.

"Just be careful. They've got me out there looking for you but I'll be sure to find some way to run this case straight into the ground," said Matthews.

Matthews got the feeling that Mercer had tuned him out as he continued to thoroughly examine his self-portraits.

"Well, I'll see you later," he said as he rose up from his chair and turned to exit the room.

"Jake's out," said Mercer, the moment that Matthews had reached the door.

"Come again?" said Matthews as he stopped dead within his tracks and turned around.

"You heard me. He finished serving his bid at the top of the year. I would have handled him but I was kind of hoping for the right person to come along and tackle the job if you know what I mean," said Mercer knowingly.

"Is he still knee deep in the game?" asked Matthews.

"No, he isn't," said Mercer as he took out a cigarette and lit it.

"What's he up to?" asked Matthews in a casual but dangerous voice.

"Apparently, he's a janitor now. I heard he's trying to get his life together, and that he's outta the game," said Mercer as he took a strong drag from his cigarette.

"I'll take care of him," said Matthews as he made his way out the door.

"And Ron, don't think I'm doing any bit of this for you, as you know, I have my own personal reasons."

"Oh, of course," he replied in a casual voice that sounded forced.

"Therefore, please stay far and out of my way. If the precinct so happens to get even a whiff about you, I'll have no choice but to do what I have to do."

And without another glance back, Matthews left Mercer in silence to ponder upon what he had meant. He then phoned up the 23rd precinct and made up a cock and bull story about not being able to return that day due to an upset stomach. Obviously, this wasn't true.

Moreover, Matthews had only gone home early to let the news of Jake Fisher's release register within his brain.

IV

The following day at the 23rd precinct, Matthews arrived bright and early as he found me finishing up a list of potential suspects.

"Good morning," I said to him the moment I noticed that he had walked into the office.

"Morning," he replied as he sat down and pried open a bag from Dunkin' Donuts.

"How are you feeling today?" I asked as I made my way over to the scanner.

"I'm fine, why do you ask?" said Matthews in between a bite of a coffee black donut.

"Because of your sickness. Didn't you have an upset stomach yesterday?" I asked as I eyed him suspiciously.

"Oh yeah, that. You know, I think it must have stemmed from what I ate the night before," said Matthews as he finished his last donut and threw the bag into the office trash can.

"Sorry to hear that man. But check this out, Gordon will be here any moment, he wants to talk about this Ron Mercer guy and so, this list that I've assembled will tell him everything he needs to know while we're out there hitting the streets."

After grabbing the documents from me and reading them over a several amount of times, Matthews handed me back the files and said, "That's great work."

Just in that moment, the door to the office had been immediately swung open.

"Good morning gentleman," said Gordon as he sat down in a chair that equally stood both six inches apart between both Matthews and my personal desk.

"Good morning to you too," I said as I gathered my files together.

"James," said Matthews as he bit into a snickers candy bar without turning around once to face the captain.

Refreshing the Mind. *To those of you who are reading our set of cases for the very first time, please bear with me as I fill you in. Also, to those of you that may be familiar with what I'm about to say, all I am doing is refreshing your memories. As far as the connection between James Gordon and Frank Matthews goes, it ranges all the way back to 1962 when they both had become detectives within the 23rd precinct. Whether you believe it or not is not of my concern, but at the time, the story goes that they had actually been very good friends. Frank Matthews had also been Captain Gordon's best man for his first marriage. However, all of that changed the moment Gordon was promoted to Captain Lieutenant of Brooklyn's 23rd precinct. Between the two, Matthews had been ranked higher and like detective Lane, was a competent and well-rounded hard-boiled cop. That all changed on the day of the promotion however, on October 19th, 1977. Matthews felt as if he had been the right man for the job; as he should have. Events such as those are what lead to him becoming the cold hearted person he became years later...and that you now see before you today.*

"Yes, well, what do you guys have for me as of now?" he asked.

"Alvin, here, compiled the list all by his lonesome James. As you know, I was under the weather yesterday and therefore, didn't have the time in aiding its construct," said Matthews as he tried to wipe the residue of chocolate marks off of his face.

"Indeed, I'm well aware," said Gordon as he stared at us.

"Okay, well first I'm going to be honest with you cap. Creating as well as assorting this list wasn't easy in the slightest. As you know, Mercer carries a record as long as the great wall of China," I said while running through the list with my thumb.

Captain Gordon gave off a smirk as he listened to my statement.

"Tell me more," he urged.

"And well, some of the names we've compiled here hold no weight in terms of his current whereabouts," I added.

"Go on," he said.

"There was a boy back in 2000 by the name of Terrance Hawkins. He was killed after word got around that he was keeping some daily revenue for himself without first forking over all initial profits to his boss."

"Give me another name," demanded Gordon as he placed his forefinger upon his recently grown mustache and pondered deep in thought.

"Then there was Cliff White who had a dispute with one of his fellow drug pushers back in 98' and when the situation escalated and had gotten too far out of control, Mercer caught up to White at Seaview Park and plugged him twice in the back of the head. White then died shortly after. I'm also sure that you'll do well to remember that White had allegedly stolen some of his fellow pusher's supply which led to Mercer terminating him."

"Yes, I do remember," said Gordon as he took out a black little notepad and scribbled some notes.

"And last, but not least, very recent to be exact, two young men that happened to be from the Flatbush area by the names of Chris Crooks and Johnny Steele were found dead in a project building laundry room. A tenant who happened to be getting ready to wash her clothes at the crack of dawn, found the bodies of the men mangled and decapitated within the machine. Let's just say that they weren't found tumble dry," I said as I crossed out names as I went along.

Realization: As Matthews continued to sit back while listening intently, he thought about the prior meeting that he had had with Mercer and wondered who had been the two guys that he had gotten rid of recently. Could they have been Chris Crooks and Johnny Steele?

"So basically, this Mercer devil punishes his workers in ways that are mostly severe if they prove to be of no use or double-cross him," said Gordon as he wrote more notes at a rapid pace.

"Precisely," I said as I made notes myself.

"These poor young boys. If only they had the proper guidance. Their daddy's were probably long gone before they could even walk," said Gordon with a tone of regret.

"Yeah and as far as the rest of these names go, they happen to be those of Crip gang members if you want them," I said.

"No need to read them, just make me a copy for my files and leave them out of your search. The last thing the BKPD needs is a bloody street war composing of the cops in black and those boys in blue," said Gordon as he scratched his head.

"I agree," I said as I got out of my seat and went to the copier to make replications of potential suspects for the captain.

"Here's what I want and expect from the both of you. I need you two to find out anything that you possibly can about Mercer's current location and his strongest connections. Once that's settled, we'll devise an operation to take down Ron Mercer and whoever that may be currently helping him. Also, as you go along, be sure to keep me posted," he said as he suddenly rose from the chair he'd been occupying.

"Not a problem cap," I said as I placed my list of suspects into a nearby folder.

"Keep in touch you too," said Gordon before shutting the office door with a loud slam.

"Listen up kid, just tell me when and where you need me to be and I'll do whatever that is expected of me. It sure looks as if you've got this whole thing situated."

"Sure thing, Frank, will do," I said, not understanding that at the time he was playing the role of clueless sheep.

"As of right now, if you'll excuse me, I'm going to head off to lunch," he said.

"Go right ahead, I'm going to do the same in a few as well. I've just got some last minute things to take care of," I said as I opened a cabinet to find some important documents.

"See you later then," said Matthews as he grabbed his coat and walked out of the office.

"Later," I replied as I extracted files from within the drawer in order to focus upon our narrowed list of suspects.

The remainder of October consisted of Matthews and I placing drug dealers and crooks into line ups which led to heavy interrogation. It was our biggest of hopes that we would be able to dig out any bits of critical information that we sought. Unfortunately, for us, no felon or hot head would speak up and tell the truth.

"C'mon for Christ's sake Mr. Scott, give us something!" I said as I brought down my fists hard upon the table that

Matthews and I had been inquiring the petty Brooklyn drug dealer.

Brandon Scott was a young man in his mid-to-late twenties that had been serving four years for violating his parole. He had a hard looking face that spoke for him living a rough life. Under his right eye was a long and visceral scar that he had received from a bar brawl in 1997. His hair was long and braided in cornrows that sat neatly upon his head.

"Listen, you filthy pigs, I'm already doing my time in here so don't think persuading me is going to get me talking. I'd rather hang myself with a belt if I was allowed to have one," he said.

"Now, listen boy, and listen good, you hear? All you have to do is just give us a couple of names here and there, in regards to Mercer and maybe, just maybe, on your next appeal there might be a possibility for a sentence reduction," said Matthews as he kept his hands within his pockets while remaining calm and collected.

"Man, y'all cop niggas just don't listen, do you? How many times do I have to say no? I ain't coming across as a snitch back in the hood. Mercer's got the entire Flatbush section as well as many other hoods in BK on lock! Any person who interferes or tries to put him down is a dead man," said Scott as he took turns in staring at the both of us.

"So you're not going to tell us anything?" I asked Scott again as I hoped that he would change his mind after waiting several minutes.

"Nope, not a goddamn thing," he said as he bit into his fingernails and looked up at me and Matthews as if we had something stuck in between our noses.

VI

"What is it about Mercer that prevents these guys from talking?" I asked Matthews as we both headed to our office about an hour after the inquiry.

"You've gotta understand, he's dangerous. I wouldn't get myself too wrapped up in his shit either if I knew that my life was at stake," said Matthews as he had withdrawn the office key from within his pocket and unlocked the door.

"Yeah, I guess you're right," I said as I followed him into the room.

"What now?" I continued as I packed my bag to head home.

"Gordon will let us know. I mean, it's not as if we haven't been knocking upon the right doors. Sometimes, you just hope that when you knock a bit harder, someone will freakin' answer," said Matthews.

VII

Later that Friday night, I found myself alone in my Bay Ridge condo watching re-runs of the Fresh Prince of Bel-Air when all of a sudden, my Nextel dispatch went off.

As I swiftly grabbed the phone from the arm rest of my cream leather couch, I looked at the screen for caller identification and saw that it was Captain Gordon.

"Hello," I said as I kept my eyes transfixed upon the television.

"Alvin, what's the latest? Anything at all?" he asked as if him dispatching my Nextel radio close to midnight was just as ordinary as going for a three p.m. power run.

"Yes and no," I replied as I finally got up and paced back and forth between the living room and my kitchen.

"What do you mean by that exactly?" he asked.

"I say yes because Matthews and I have gone back and forth in terms of snatching up dealers off of the streets and questioning them inside the interrogation room as of late. But at the same time, I also say no because everyone seems afraid to talk. No one wants to quote-on-quote *snitch* on Mercer in fear of what he may possibly do to them. Even the inmates within Rikers or Brooklyn Bay have failed to cooperate and divulge such vital information."

"Well that's understandable don't you think? I mean, imagine snitching on Mercer and you've just been released five years later to find out that everyone from the mother of your kids to your grandmother is dead," said Gordon in a matter-of-fact tone.

113

"You're right, it does happen on the daily," I said as I returned to the couch.

"How is Matthews helping you through everything?" asked Gordon more seriously.

"He's been great, a huge help I would say. He told me earlier while on the way out that he would inform you of our difficulties."

"I haven't heard a damn thing from that guy since the day that we all sat down and had our initial chat. Do me a favor will you? Make sure that Matthews is active and thoroughly engaged because this is usually the time when he tends to lose focus the moment he recognizes that a case is going cold," said Captain Gordon in a serious tone.

"No need to worry cap, I can assure you that Matthews is as determined and as focused as I am. Believe me," I said as I turned off the television and headed towards the bedroom.

"Well, alright, I'll see you during the week," said Gordon.

"See you," he said.

"Goodnight," I answered before ending the dispatch call.

As I glanced at the alarm clock the moment that I had gotten into bed, I noticed that it was twenty past midnight which meant that Halloween had officially arrived. Before dozing off and heading to sleep, I made a note to remind myself to call Matthews and as well as buy candy for trick-or-treaters in the morning. And with that final thought etched upon the surface of my brain, I plopped my head upon the pillow and immediately fell into a deep sleep.

VIII

The next day, I remained true to my word as I dialed up Matthews' dispatch.

"Hello?" he said after about four beeps.

"Frank, how are you? Fine I hope."

"Yeah, yeah, I'm alright. What's up?"

"Nothing much, I'm just a little on edge about this case right now, that's all."

"Well, don't worry about it kid. Sometimes you tend to stress yourself out when dealing with work and stuff," said Matthews as he stated the obvious.

"Ummm, Frank?" I said as I prepared to tell him that Gordon had asked me about him sustaining focus.

"Yeah, kid?" he responded in a dull kind of voice.

"Never mind. See you on Monday."

"Monday, it is," replied Frank.

"Yeah, Monday," I said in finality.

"Monday," said Frank before finally hanging up.

IX

"What a cuckoo," said Matthews as he rose up from his couch and exited out the door.

As Matthews got into his car and drove down the street, he heard the sound of thunder cackling from a distance.

The winds were strong and the clouds were a dark gray. Moreover, the more Matthews drove; he noticed that at any moment, Brooklyn would be instantaneously drenched with rain. As he continued to drive, he watched people without umbrellas immediately run for shelter. It wasn't until Matthews had reached his destination on Beverley Road when the rain finally began to pour down as if they were oversized tear drops.

Before getting out of his car, Matthews pulled a ski mask over his head which fittingly accompanied his umbrella. He then popped open his trunk and extracted from it, a miniscule baseball bat in which he placed within his inner coat pocket. And after several movements of battling harsh raging winds, he finally made his way into the housing complex that he had been eyeing for about a week.

MERCY FOR MURDER: *The more Matthews climbed the dark staircases of the building, the more he did his absolute best to* *remain as silent as he possibly could. Upon reaching the seventh floor, he checked his watch to see that it was approximately 10:19pm. He knew that the person he was searching for lived in one of the floor's apartments. After two weeks of threats and the promising to murder innocent people's families, Matthews had gotten word that Jake Fisher lived on the seventh floor of the Beverley housing complex.*

When Matthews reached apartment 709, he knocked upon the door with a hard fist several times before leaning to the side of its entrance.

"What are these trick-or-treaters doing out so late?" asked Jake Fisher from within the apartment as he muted the sound of his television set.

As he heard Jake approaching the door, Matthews quickly slipped on dark leather gloves that covered his thick and long hands. He also had placed his left hand within his trench coat as he waited patiently. It would only be a few seconds later when the door had finally unlocked and a creak had sounded to signify it becoming ajar.

"Listen, it's really late and there's no more candy for you kids to be—"said Jake as he narrowly avoided the brutal collision of Matthews' twin barrel .45.

As fast as he could, Jake ran into his kitchen and picked up a silver shining meat cleaver that possessed a brass wooden handle.

He then swung the object diagonally several times but missed as Matthews dodged with the grace of a twenty-something trapped within a middle-aged man's body.

After failing to strike with every attempt, Jake then ran into the living room and opened his window which led out onto the fire escape.

He had one foot upon the ledge and one that was halfway out until he was then grabbed by Matthews who reeled him in like a fisherman and threw him upon the floor.

Matthews then proceeded to kick Fisher several times in the face before he looked all around and found what he had been searching for. After picking up the meat cleaver, he brought it down hard upon Fisher's right leg.

A blood curling scream pierced the night as the thunder continued to rumble and clap in the distance.

Blood had begun to ooze throughout the tiled floor, when Matthews took out his bat and began to swing down hard upon Jake's body. After what seemed like five minutes of crunching and forceful blows, Matthews had finally stopped his infliction of pain. He was sure that the man who ratted out his nephew eight years prior was now dead.

Before leaving the apartment, he fully opened the window that Jake had tried to escape from in order to create a misconception of the murderer having fled through it. Just as he was halfway towards the exit, he heard what seemed like a strong gasping for air and the faint calling of a name.

"Luke, Luke, Luke, Luke…" said the faint voice of Jacob Fisher.

Matthews slowly turned around and walked back to where Fisher lay numb in excruciating pain.

The moment that Matthews was in close range, he was able to soak in all of the damage that he had done. Within that moment, Matthews took off his ski-mask and peered into the hopeless eyes of Jake Fisher.

Jake Fisher was heavily battered and crushed as several of his bones stuck out in grisly fashion. It was a gruesome sight as Jake was completely unrecognizable while drenched in his own blood.

Although he was close to death, Jake expressed an unmistaken look of horror and fear as Matthews simply smiled a frank but twisted smile.

As his smile faded, it was then that Matthews suddenly remembered Jake's meat cleaver which lied several feet away from him.

After several moments of observing it, Matthews walked over and picked it up. He then returned to where Fisher lied and started to bring it down hard upon his crushed and mangled body. For each crushing blow, Matthews repetitively kept raising the meat cleaver until he no longer had the strength for the job…

When Matthews entered the street, he looked up at the window that contained the body of a now deceased Jake Fisher. As he watched the rain beat hard upon it, a huge sudden flash of lightning brightened up the darkened gray sky. Within minutes of motioning to his vehicle, the Halloween rain became so fierce that it was impossible for him to see cars as he walked along Brooklyn's dark and narrowed streets. But as he finally entered his 1982 Honda Accord, Matthews couldn't resist taking pride in that the job had been done.

Episode 6:

"Also for Mercer"

I

The moment Matthews returned to his Brownsville apartment, the first thing he did was clean himself up. After a well needed shower, he then left and returned minutes later with a black and large garbage bag in which to deposit his all black Halloween outfit into. He then decided to step out again as he drove to pier 96 in Coney Island and walked the boardwalk. As he made it to the edge of the beach with the rain pouring harder than ever, he threw the bag into the waters and watched the force of the rain and wind, carry it away from shore.

When he was sure that the bag had gone below surface level view, he hastily walked back to his car and returned home. Upon reaching his residence, he wasted no time by changing into something dry and comfortable before heading to sleep.

II

The following evening, Matthews had been in his apartment eating a bowl of ramen noodle soup while watching the Simpsons when his dispatcher went off.

"Yeah," he said in a lazy voice as he casually picked his nose.

"Matthews, sorry to disturb," said Gordon in a rare, sleepy voice.

"Yeah," Matthews repeated.

"Hey, listen, do you happen to know detective Luke Fisher of the burglary department?"

"Yeah, he works very closely with detective Lane," said Matthews bluntly.

"Yes, well, I'm very sorry to inform you of this, but, his brother was murdered last night in his apartment. We're still trying to figure it all out as we speak. Many things regarding the crime are still very premature."

"Oh my God, I feel so bad for the guy. I'm deeply sorry to hear that," lied Matthews as he picked up the remote and decided to change the channel.

"I agree, very, very, sad indeed, which is why I want you on the case as lead detective accompanying Fisher in his pursuit to find those responsible for the crime."

"Correct me if I'm wrong here James, but don't you want me to track down Mercer with Alvin at the moment?"

"Yes, I do, but I'm well aware that you can't be in both places at once. Therefore, I've assigned detective Williams of burglary and narcotics to continue that case with Alvin instead, while you handle this one. Therefore, you two will be doing a flip flop from the two departments," said Gordon.

"Not a problem then. Starting next week I'll get right to it," said Matthews as he displayed a twisted smile behind the phone's speaker.

"Good, I want you to be at the apartment early tomorrow morning as we make record of the scene," said Gordon.

"Sure, I'll be there," replied Matthews.

"Do you need the address of the apartment?"

"No, it's okay, I'll just ring up Luke Fisher and get it from him," lied Matthews once again.

"Oh and Frank? Be very delicate and kind with Luke during this stressful time, okay? I'm sure that even someone such as yourself can imagine how he's feeling," said Gordon.

"But of course," he replied, "see you tomorrow."

"See you then," said Gordon just before ending the conversation.

No Case: *The moment Frank Matthews hung up the dispatch, he knew that the upcoming weeks and months would probably be the most frustrating time for the 23rd precinct. After all, it was he who had killed Jake Fisher, it was he who had put him behind bars once I had realized that someone solely within Bed-Stuy had murdered Evan Wright.*

As Matthews prepared to go to bed, he decided upon making the upcoming adventure his very last case. After years of covering up his entire track record, he finally came to terms with being tired of it all. He was now approaching his late sixties and deep down within his rotten heart, he knew that the more he played such games, there would never be a solid chance of him living to see seventy.

III

On Monday morning, Matthews arrived at the scene of the crime at approximately seven a.m.

As he made his way onto the seventh floor and into the very apartment that he had murdered Jake Fisher in just only days before, he was surprisingly taken aback by what he had found.
As he recalled, Jake was left soaking in his own blood on the brown tiled floor and so he was surprised to see Jake Fisher's body lying lifeless on the sofa with three bullet wounds accompanying his now tattered head. Simply put, someone else had come after he had departed to finish the job.

Detective Matthews then walked into the kitchen where the 23rd precinct crime lab team were scattered all around its vicinity frantically placing all of the evidence that they could find within mini plastic bags. When detective Matthews had exited the kitchen and re-entered the living room, he noticed that detective Fisher had now arrived and was observing his brother closely as he tried to fight back tears.

"We're going to find out who did this to him Fisher. Mark my words," said Matthews as he had uncharacteristically placed a hand upon Luke Fisher's shoulder.

"I know that we hadn't seen eye to eye recently, but he was still my brother, you know?" said Fisher as he wiped off tears that had been rolling down his cheeks.

"Yes, I understand. That's why I was so eager to take this case. Homicide is my field of expertise and believe me when I say that I have always had the upmost respect for you Fisher."

"I truly appreciate that Matthews. You see, he did about eight years for a drug bust back in 93' and had just been released," said Fisher in an unusual raspy voice that wasn't his own.

As paranoid as he was about his cover, Matthews quickly tried to change the subject.

"You know, this is it for me?" said Matthews as he gaped out of the apartment window that he had only looked out of two nights prior.

"What is?" asked Fisher.

"I'm sixty-five now, and my pension will be kicking in soon. It's time for me to call it quits. However, I thought nothing would be better than helping out a detective in whom I truly respect just before hanging it up."

"That means a lot to me Matthews but if you'll excuse me, I'm heading outside to see if the medical examiner has arrived."

"Go right ahead," said Matthews, "I'm going to browse around a bit more to see if the suspect might have left anything of value."

As both men nodded mutually in agreement, detective Matthews exhaled when he saw that Fisher had finally left the apartment. He then returned to the window as he saw Luke Fisher talking to Captain Gordon who had just then arrived on the concrete below.

"Just a little bit more of a performance Frank and you'll be in the clear," he muttered under his breath as he stepped away from the window while surveying the scene.

After meeting with Captain Gordon and detective Fisher briefly before heading home, Matthews had thought about visiting Ron Mercer. Deep down inside, however, he knew that it was a bad idea. Tension in Brooklyn was at an all-time high and with the case that he had just been given, and as well as the case that Williams and I were left to finish, he knew that rogue visitations were certainly out of the question.

And so, that night, he decided to take a trip to the Trash Bar...

IV

"Frankie," said Tim, the bartender with a grin as he noticed Matthews approaching the counter.

"Nothing tonight, Timmy. I would just like to use your phone," answered Matthews, as his face showed that he meant business.

"Oh sure," said Tim, obviously taken aback by Matthews' uptightness.

And without another word Matthews walked his way over to the bar's public phone.

After removing the receiver off of the wall jack, Matthews then took out a tiny sheet of paper that had a number scribbled upon it.

A few rings after dialing, anxiety subsided in Matthews as the voice of Ron Mercer had come onto the phone.

"Who is it?" he asked.

"Big Matt," replied Matthews.

"Damn Matt, it's almost midnight, what's up?" he asked.

"Three bullet wounds to the forehead of Jake Fisher, that's what," responded Matthews in a snarl.

"Yeah, you like that huh?" said Mercer in an amused and cruel voice.

"No, why did you do that?" asked Matthews.

"Easy, easy there, big Matt. By the time I got there, a majority of the job had already been done."

"What do you mean?" asked Matthews very impatiently.

"Fisher was still alive when I got there. Whoever that took care of him did a hell of a job."

"I did that," said Matthews with a sneer.

"Wow, Matt, amazing. You know, I wasn't sure if you had gone through with it which is why I decided to do it myself."

"You mean, he was still breathing when you found him?"

"Yeah, but just barely. He had just finished crawling out of his front door."

"Well listen, it's done, so please stay far away from it, Mercer. They've put me on this case now but by no means have they closed yours. You would do best to take care of yourself," warned Matthews.

"I know everything will be fine Matt, especially with you at the helm," he said confidently.

"No, it won't. My life and career are at stake too," said Matthews.

"Well, whose fault is that?" said Mercer as his voice abruptly turned cold.

"Listen to me you East Flatbush piece of shit. I don't know how religious you are but you'd better pray that you and I don't get linked to this murder wrap because if we do, I just may have to kill you," said Matthews straight-forwardly.

An awkward silence had then ensued to the point where both men thought the phone line to be dead.

"You still there?" asked Matthews.

"Yeah," said Mercer hesitantly.

"Stay out of the way, are we clear?" he asked.

"Yeah, clear," said Mercer as his voice sounded weaker than usual.

"Good," said Matthews as he then hung up the phone.

He then returned to the bar and wished Tim a goodnight before heading home.

Detective Matthews knew that he had to get some rest. The following morning would be the commencing of a very stressful case.

The luck of detective Matthews seemed to have worsened upon arriving at the 23rd precinct, the following day. Immediately after entering the office, he found out that detective Deborah Lane, a competent and hard-boiled cop from the burglary department, had also been assigned to Jake Fisher's case. Within a few minutes of letting it all sink in, Matthews had to come to the realization that he shouldn't have been surprised. Detective Fisher had been Lane's partner for the past six years barring a few cases as the only exceptions. But when Gordon had made Matthews the head of the operation, he should have immediately understood that the possibility of Lane joining the team was extremely high.

A few hours later after collectively compiling leads and possible informants for the case, a medical examiner that frequently collaborated with the homicide department by the name of Paul Sanders walked into the office. Sanders had a list of files and papers jammed in between both of his hands.

"I noticed some things last night that I thought I would share," he said once he had settled in and organized all of the files upon Matthews' desk.

One good look at Paul Sanders and you could instantly tell that his body type exhibited him of being within the wrong profession. He stood at about six foot four, had long and lengthy arms and was definitely packing some muscle underneath his white garments. As he ruffled his sandy brown hair while picking up the first few sheets of paper that contained dire information regarding the case, Lane displayed that she wasn't abashed at being the first to speak.

"Talk to us Dr. Sanders, what do you have?" she asked.

"From last night's investigation while working with coroner Murray, we discovered that the killer wore leather gloves and used some kind of powerful object to fracture the right side of the victim's skull."

Before continuing any further, he then placed the sheets of files back onto the table as he picked up another set of files that he had brought into the office.

"We couldn't find any fingerprints around the apartment but we're heavily leaning towards objects such as a hammer or baseball bat that would've had the forceful ability to leave the victim in the gruesome state that he was found in."

Once again, Sanders placed some of those files back against the table as he picked up a final set and held them neatly within his hands.

"And last, but not least, Jake's apartment window in the living room was left open. Now, although the window may have already been open ajar before the suspect even got there, it makes more sense to believe that he opened it just before fleeing the scene in order to fool investigators. I mean, it was Halloween night for Christ's sake. I'm sure Fisher wasn't trying to receive some fresh air in forty-six degree weather."

"Yeah, you're right," said detective Fisher.

"Anything else?" he asked earnestly.

"No, that's all we have for now I'm afraid. But if anything happens to come up, I'll be sure to have you all come down to the lab," said Dr. Sanders.

"Thank you Dr. Sanders, we'll be in touch," said Matthews.

"Not a problem. If you all have any further questions, please, don't hesitate to ask," he replied.

The three detectives were once again left alone as Dr. Sanders had gathered all of his files and swiftly made his way to the medical department.

"Let's get out and hit the streets. It's time to start pressing all of the drug pushers and arms dealers of Brooklyn and NYC for that matter," said Matthews with a rare inflection of leadership hidden just beneath his actual voice.

"No disrespect detective, but I think our first course of action would be to talk to Jake's former friends, associates and anyone he's been in contact with over the past few years. Besides, the landscape of the city has changed and many of the dealers that Jake used to mess with are no longer around," said Lane simply stating out the obvious.

At that precise moment, Matthews face flushed into a putrid red.

"I don't tell you how to do your job Ms. Lane and so I'd like it if you wouldn't advise me on how to do mine," barked Matthews in a sharp voice.

Detective Lane was on the cusp of responding to Matthews' statement when Fisher, sensing tension cut in, "Look if there's anyone who would provide us with a great start, I'd say it would have to be his girlfriend. Her name is Tanya Watson. She lives on Beverley as well, not too far from his old apartment building. She happened to know all of his friends, where he worked, she's definitely a start," said Fisher as he stared at both detectives and hoped that their quarreling would cease.

"Then let's get over there and quickly, we're moving too slow," said Lane as she put on her black BKPD jacket and left the office.

Extra Caution: *There was no doubt in Matthews' mind on why Fisher enjoyed working with Deborah Lane. Firstly, above all else, she was a no-nonsense kind of a person. Without question, she most certainly got things done which reflected in her good standing at the 23rd precinct and lastly, on a personal note, she reminded Matthews of himself back when he was an honorable* *detective solving cases with force but at the time, going about them the right way. Therefore, he knew that with her, he had to tread lightly and proceed with extra caution. But for some reason, deep down inside, he didn't think that she would have him figured out. In his mind, all that he had to do was make it past the next three months safe and sound; and he was certain that he'd be able to do just that.*

"*I mean, I'm Matthews for pete's sake,*" he thought to himself as he followed the detectives out of the office.

VII

By Tuesday, detective Fisher realized that he had learned more about his brother in those past two days than he had over the last ten years. All of the information that the three detectives had gathered were stepping stones that they hoped would lead to them finding Jake Fisher's killer.

It wasn't until later that morning when detective Matthews walked into detective Lane's office and spotted her in deep conversation with Luke Fisher.

"Anything besides what we've learned?" he asked.

Matthews' Inner Conscience: *This was a question that needed no response. All he had to do was keep the heat away from him. He knew that it would only be a matter of time.*

"Nope," replied Fisher in a heavily frustrated voice.

"The pool hall that Mr. Demarco told us about is open from Wednesday to Saturday," said Lane after Matthews had taken a seat facing them in the far left corner of the office.

"Tomorrow, we're going to go check it out," she added.

"Sounds good, but I was thinking that we should go there on Thursday or Friday instead," replied Matthews.

"Matthews, it's open tomorrow. The sooner we can nail solid leads and answers, the better it will be for us," pressed Fisher.

"I understand kid but anyone involved with the crime or informants that may have known Jake wouldn't be showing up to a place like that with his death being so sudden," said Matthews defensively.

"Look, we're going tomorrow and that's all there is to it. The first ninety-six hours of a case are critical when assembling as much evidence as possible. A senior detective most certainly knows that. Especially one within the homicide department, Frank," said Lane.

The two of them had been clashing ever since the case had started. They were only two days in and it had obviously become a battle of wills. Matthews had then raised both of his hands in the air as if he was expecting to get frisked at any moment.

"Alright, it was only a suggestion. I'll see the both of you tomorrow, then," he said as he tried his hardest to suppress the vexations within him.

Keeping Cool: *Matthews was trying his best to conceal his frustration. He refused to allow detective Lane, a woman who was rightfully only doing her job, see the erratic and psychotic side of him that deep down, he had always known was there.*

"Gordon gave me the day off to plan all of my moving affairs. I've already told Fisher here that once this case is over, I'm gone," said Matthews to Lane.

"See you at the pool hall tomorrow afternoon. Two p.m.," said Fisher as he went back to typing a document on his computer.

Matthews nodded in reply to express that he understood and without another word, left the precinct to salvage the few remaining hours that were left in the day.

As he made his way into the parking garage to where his 1982 Honda Accord stood, he finally came to terms with the real reasons as to why he wanted to avoid the pool hall on Wednesday. First and foremost, he was feeling paranoid. He had been the one who murdered Jake Fisher on a chilly Halloween night within the solitude of the man's apartment. Secondly, he wanted to keep tabs on Mercer so that he could place the wrap on him whenever the time was right. Matthews had made plans to interrogate the servants of the underworld throughout Wednesday in its entirety so that he would be able to keep up with Ron Mercer's schedule.

"But all of that will have to wait until Thursday or Friday," he thought.

The following day he would go on to have a date at a pool hall with two detectives.

VIII

Jibbs Lane happened to be located between Bedford and Ocean Avenue. The following evening, all three of the detectives met up in front of the establishment and entered the cluttered hall. There was a heavy level of chatter as well as distinct clanking of pocket balls.

The three detectives then approached a heavy set man at the main counter who looked as if he beat his wife on the nights that he didn't come home sober. His eyes were a bloodshot red and were supported by bags the size of thumbs. His bald head glistened as the hall's ceiling lights centered upon his thick fat head.

"Can I help you?" he asked grumpily as he took in all of their appearances.

"Yeah, do you run this place?" asked Fisher as he surveyed the scene before placing his forearms upon the man's counter.

"Yeah, what is it that you need?" he asked gruffly as he eyed them with suspicion.

"We're with the Brooklyn police department," said Lane as she hoisted a golden shield from one of the pockets of her jacket.

"How can I be of help officers?" the man then asked nervously.

Upon seeing detective Lane's badge, the owner of Jibbs had swiftly changed his demeanor.

"We're looking for three fellas who come around here sometimes. Their names are Smoke, Jeff, and Trey. Maybe you know them perhaps?" asked Fisher in a tone that displayed rhetoric.

"Of course, they're regulars. They're here on most nights. In fact, they're right over there!" he said.

As he positioned himself to the point where he was able to lean over the counter, the Jibbs owner, who they later found out was named Stanley Brown, pinpointed three young black males who appeared to be in their late twenties.

They were all gathered at the pool table obsessively chatting and cackling while in the midst of a game.

"Thanks, that will be all," said Lane just before they traveled to the table of Smoke, Jeff and Trey.

The moment that detectives Matthews, Lane and Fisher had reached the pool table of the men soon-to-be in questioning, activity ceased immediately as they all looked up in silence.

"BKPD," said Matthews as he flashed his badge while the men took in his appearance.

"I hear you guys happen to know Jake," he then said as he picked up a pool stick and hit a pocket ball right down the middle.

"Yeah, he's a cool guy. We often get into a game of two's whenever he's here," said the man who stood in the middle of the three.

He stood around a solid six foot two with dark brown hair, thick black eyebrows and a deep bass of a voice which was an inner-city Brooklyn accent from the moment he had opened his mouth.

"Well, he's dead. He died late last Saturday night by means of a homicide. Do you guys happen to know anything about that?" asked Fisher in a stern manner.

"Oh shit, Jake Fish? Damn, he was definitely worried about his own well-being as of late," said the guy who had spoken last.

"Who are you? If you don't mind me asking," said Lane.

"They call me Smoke but my real name is Bernard Robinson," he said.

As the three detectives observed him some more, they quickly began to understand why Robinson was nicknamed Smoke. His lips had been so black that many could have assumed that he smoked charcoal.

"Say, do you three mind coming in for questioning downtown?" asked Fisher.

"No, not at all. We were all on good terms with Jake. Anything that we could do to help is fine," said Smoke as he looked at Jeff and Trey for reassurance in which they both had nodded.

IX

Back at the 23ʳᵈ precinct on Parkside Avenue, the three detectives had split up in order to interrogate each of the pool players individually. Detective Fisher took Smoke, also known as Bernard, into his office, Lane interviewed Jeff in hers and Matthews had taken on the assignment of interviewing Trey. After sitting Trey down for about what was half an hour to where Matthews had only gone as far as asking him his full name, he then asked Trey whether he had ever heard of a Ron Mercer.

"Yeah man. I mean shit, everybody in the hood knows about big Ron."

"It seems like you and Ron go way back my man. I'm sorry, did I just hear you refer to him as *big* Ron?" asked Matthews inquisitively.

"Yeah, well, when I was a little kid, Ron used to be a young dealer on my block during the late seventies into the early eighties back in Marcy and that's what they used to call him," said Trey as he scratched his head.

"Where can I find him?" asked Matthews as he lowered his voice.

"Last I heard, he was in Red Hook, but some of the people that I talk to say that they last seen him in Midwood. Not too far off exactly from Brooklyn College within the backstreet of Kenilworth place.

"You're free to go," said Matthews as he abruptly ended the interrogation.

X

Another half an hour later, Matthews had reconvened with both detectives Lane and Fisher in front of their office.

"Wasn't there that night. Everything he told me was redundant and similar to our previous questioning of Mr. Demarco and little Ms. Watson," said Matthews.

"The only name and possible lead we have is some guy named Ron Mercer. Mercer…Mercer…why does that name sound so familiar? Where have I heard it before?" asked Fisher as the curiosity was plainly visible from the throbbing veins that danced upon his forehead.

Matthews had noticed that Lane was deep in thought as well, but when she had finally said nothing, he decided it was best that he too, did the same.

"You know," said Lane, as if she had come across a sudden realization.

"Please, don't. No, no, no," thought Matthews.

"That name does sound vaguely familiar for some reason," she continued.

"It's getting late, why don't we just pick it up tomorrow?" asked Matthews as he abruptly changed the subject.

He was actually worried for once but tried his absolute best to keep it hidden.

The three detectives had all mutually agreed and went about their separate ways.

XI

The following day brought along the city's first snow shower of the season as light flakes of white began to cover the entire borough of Brooklyn.

As detectives Lane, Fisher and Matthews spent another day working on the case, they now decided to focus their attention on locating the whereabouts of Ron Mercer. They decided that finding Mercer, (whether he was guilty or not) would open up the case to the point of solidifying an exact lead all while pinpointing them in the right direction.

It was then around five p.m. when the detectives decided to call it quits for the day.

"Okay, tomorrow, I would like for us to start in Canarsie and from there we can work our way throughout all of the ghettos and corrupt places in Brooklyn," said Lane.

"Sounds great to me," said Fisher, "hopefully we can finally turn the page on this thing and actually start piecing this puzzle. I mean, we've got the pieces now," he added.

"There's a good mentality," said Matthews as he quickly fastened the buttons upon his trench coat as the three of them had risen simultaneously to leave Lane's office.

"Meet us at East 95th tomorrow Frank. It's just two blocks off from where I used to live. We're going to begin our search of the entire borough for Mercer there," said Fisher as he grabbed his bag to follow the two detectives out of the room.

"Not a problem. I'll see the two of you then bright and early," said Matthews as he stopped by his office before heading to the parking garage.

Upon reaching his Honda Accord, he wasted no time in firing up his ignition and headed home.

XII

Murder of Mercer: Frank Matthews left his Brownsville apartment around nine p.m. as he traveled towards the Midwood section of Flatbush, Brooklyn.

As he drove down the dirty and slushy streets, he realized that he had to drive cautiously due to the thick coating of snow that was smacking the windshields of his car as he cruised along.

After coming across an abandoned old building on Kenilworth place, he decided that he would give it a look-see in order to find who he had been searching for.

Matthews made sure to put on a pair of black leather gloves that went well with his face mask and the rest of his outfit. He also had on his black Nike sneakers with its traditional swoosh logo emblazoned upon its side.

As he made his way into the building, he made sure to check every floor in order to be certain of its vacancy. It wasn't until he was climbing up the steps of the sixth and final floor when he heard voices approaching the location in which he currently stood.

"I dunno, what do you think Ron's gonna do?" asked a clear and distinct voice.

"I'm not sure, but I've honestly never seen him so shaken up before in my life. This Matthews guy or whatever his name is must be a true O.G.," said a second voice.

"For sure, I mean, my cousin D-Mack been knowin' Ron since the seventies and he says that no man has ever been able to put fear within his heart like that."

"Shit, that's wild right there," said the second voice.

"Excuse me, fellas," said Matthews as the two young men had now come into distinct view.

They then instantly responded by pulling out guns.

"Hey, I come in peace. I'm a nice guy, really," said Matthews as he stared them both in the eyes and saw the fear that they contained.

"What do you want?" said the first guy who was really thin with dark, black skin and a sallow face.

"I'm looking for old Ronnie. He's a friend of mine," said Matthews as he slowly began to advance towards the two young men.

"That's as close as you're gonna get brother or I'll have no choice but to blow your fuckin' brains out," said the second young man.

Unlike the first guy, he was really thick and had rolls under his chin. There was no doubt that he missed one or two gym classes within his youth.

Matthews then proceeded to climb up the stairs as if he hadn't heard them. There was a hungry look in his eye that he rarely, if ever, displayed.

"Let this be a lesson to you, next time you have a gun big boy, be sure to use it."

And without warning, Matthews inserted a switch blade hard into his belly.

The chubby kid then stared in complete horror as he began to see nothing but red oozing upon his shirt.

Due to fright, the first kid aimed for Matthews but before pulling the trigger, Matthews had thrown him all the way down the stairs as his gun went flying into the air.

As it landed upon the floor, the boy quickly ran for it when Matthews had decided to pull out his own .38 and shot him four times in the back. The boy then crumpled dead upon the ground before becoming an instant oozing Jacuzzi bath of blood.

Without hesitation, he casually went onto the sixth floor where he saw a door with dim lighting from within that flickered faintly beyond its surface.

"Shhhh, somebody's coming I tell you. Didn't you hear those gunshots?" said a voice that sounded familiar.

"Maybe Tyshawn and Rohan took care of whoever that was on their way up here," said a second and familiar voice.

"Wait, wait, I hear something," said the first voice.

Matthews had then come to a complete halt when he finally began to knock upon the door.

"Who is it?" said the second voice.

In an instant, Matthews kicked the door open with such a force that whoever had been standing directly behind it fell upon the floor and was now out cold.

As he made his way into the apartment, he noticed that it was Clay, the kid who Mercer had recently hired when he had last placed Mercer a visit. By the looks of it, his nose looked badly damaged as Matthews was sure that it had been broken. He then advanced further into the apartment when the kid named Gee, (who he had body slammed upon their last encounter) came flying out of the kitchen with a butcher's knife. Upon seeing that it was Matthews, he stopped dead in his tracks and raised both of his hands into the air as the eating utensil fell onto the floor with a sudden loud clank.

Matthews began to carve out a crooked smile as he kept his gun pointed at Gee who then began to slowly retreat into the back room.

"Wise choice kid, yes, a very wise choice, indeed," whispered Matthews as Gee kept his gaze before dissolving into the darkness.

As he made his way past Gee, he opened the door of Mercer's bedroom where he saw him attempting to climb out of the window.

Matthews wasted no time in cocking back his revolver and without warning, shot Mercer twice in the leg.

Ron Mercer then reacted to the gun wounds by letting out a huge yelp of pain.

"You're not going anywhere," said Matthews.

"We're going for a nice little ride down to the island," he added menacingly.

As he handcuffed Mercer and stuffed his mouth with a handkerchief, he walked out of the apartment and made his way back into his car.

By the time they had left the building, Matthews noticed that Gee and Clay were long gone.

As he stuffed Mercer into the backseat, he hoped that he had scared them straight. If they noticed what he had done to the guys along the stairway, it would have been evident that the lifestyle they had been sucked into was certainly not for them.

XIII

Almost forty minutes later, Matthews had made it onto the boardwalk of Coney Island. As he dragged Mercer along, it was getting difficult for him to see as the snow thickened and came down harder than ever. Christmas hadn't even arrived and yet the entire city of New York had been hit with a blizzard.

One look at Mercer and someone just had to feel bad for him. Matthews had stripped him naked; had his mouth gagged and now had him blind-folded.

The moment they had reached the edge of the pier, Matthews leaned him against the railing and said: "Any last words?"

In which Mercer responded with a strangled muffle and an obvious plead for mercy.

Without any further hesitation, Matthews threw him overboard and watched just as his naked body finally connected with the water's freezing temperatures.

After heaving a huge sigh of relief, Matthews fought to make it back to his car within the dense thickness of burgeoning snow. It was finally over...or for his sake...at least he thought it was...

XIV

The investigation upon the murder of Jake Fisher persisted for an additional two months when detective Lane decided to pop into Matthews' office on Valentine's Day.

"Come in," said Matthews as soon as he had heard a knock.

He had been sitting alone in his office watching porn but immediately turned off the computer screen as detective Lane walked in.

"What were you doing?" she asked.

"Oh, nothing. Just working on some stuff regarding the case," he said as he spun his chair so that he could face her.

"You wanna sit?"

"No, I'm actually on my way to see Captain Gordon. You know, it's funny that you mention the case because I've been having a hard time figuring some stuff out," she said in what seemed to be a straight and hardened voice.

"Oh yeah?" said Matthews apparently amused.

"Yes," she responded. "You see, I find it very odd that we've interrogated about two hundred people in not only Brooklyn, but New York City in general and we still haven't been able to find any leads."

"Yes, I find that quite baffling," said Matthews as he took a sip of tea in the mug that sat right behind the computer in which he had been watching his porn on.

"Also, I just realized that the day me and Luke had been conversing with the captain about our crossfires case, I remember that you had walked into my office as you were handed files and photos of Ron Mercer," she now said with deep concentration.

As Matthews placed his mug back onto the desk he stared at Lane while listening intently. He didn't dare look away from her now.

"That means," she continued as they made intense eye contact.

It was almost as if it had become a battle of wills between them both.

"You knew exactly who we were talking about after we had interrogated Smoke, Jeff and Trey from the pool hall. And if I also recall properly, you didn't want to go to the pool hall the first day we originally planned to. So with that being said, can you please tell me why that was?"

Matthews then chuckled before picking up the mug again and taking yet another sip of his tea.

"You're a competent detective, Deborah, but I think you may be taking things a wee bit out of proportion here," said Matthews as he had hoped to restore his cool and regain some of his mojo.

"Chauncey Matthews," she then said.

There was no doubt that Frank Matthews had given her his complete undivided attention.

"The story goes that back in 93' you and detective Alvin were on a case to find the killer of a kid named Evan Wright. But that case was closed with the arrest of Jake Fisher right? Now, I'm not saying that Jake wasn't deserving of his time, but you and I both know that he didn't kill Wright. Besides, why would he? They worked together. Also, Jake Fisher was the one who name dropped Chauncey to the D.A. in order to get reduced time on his sentence. And so, Mercer comes into play because once Jake was being questioned by the D.A. he came clean. He named as much names as possible that had been linked to Mercer, with Chauncey being one of them. Lastly, if I'm not mistaken, he had been your nephew right? I mean the whole 23rd precinct knows that... You know Frank; all of this has me wondering upon whether Jake Fisher's death was premeditated murder; and if the disappearance of Ron Mercer has any linkage to it?"

After Matthews had simply looked at her without even blinking, detective Lane simply unlocked the door and had one hand firmly grasped upon its knob.

"I'm heading out now. I'll see you tomorrow as it's almost five. I'll be sure to speak to Captain Gordon and detective Fisher as soon as I reach home," she said.

And without another word, she left detective Matthews to his thoughts as he continued to stare at the door with his mouth gapingly wide. A story that had certainly been ten years in the making had now come to a complete end as its awry conclusion manufactured the stupid look that now rested upon detective Frank Matthews' face.

Episode 7:

"Frank's Flight"

I

As detective Frank Matthews left the vicinity of the 23rd precinct, it was obvious and apparent that he was extremely flustered. The fact that Deborah Lane had pieced together the peculiar bits of information surrounding Ron Mercer had been of no surprise to him. As much as he hated to admit it, Frank Matthews knew that detective Deborah Lane was a competent and witty detective. And so, with a glance at his Casio watch, Matthews noticed that it was five o'clock as he hastily made his way to his 1982 Honda Accord.

Upon reaching it, he briefly leaned his head beside the car door as he contemplated his next move. Should he stay and complete the case? Or should he go? Those were really his only two options. If he left, he'd leave behind a trail of what he committed but would escape the clutches of the BKPD, and if he stayed put, Lane would surely do him in.

"Why I am even thinking about this?" he asked himself.

"There's no one to put the wrap on this time. If I stay here, I risk getting caught while little miss know-it-all buries me under the prison," he said as he continued to talk to himself.

Detective Matthews knew that he himself was crazy, but at the same time, he wasn't dumb. He would be taking a huge risk on staying back and working a case that he knew was dead in the water.

As he entered his Honda and fired up its engine, he swiftly made his way back to his Brownsville apartment.

To him, it was settled. He no longer worked for Parkside Avenue's 23rd precinct and his name was no longer Frank Matthews. Instead, he would go by a new name, Matt Frank. To anyone else, the mere thought of such a name would be asking for trouble, but to someone as twisted and psychotic as Matthews was, it was pure genius.

II

Matthews quickly came to an abrupt halt upon reaching his project building. He then got out of his car in hasty fashion and made his way into his apartment on the fifth floor.

The moment he was inside of his condo, the first thing Frank did was gather his most important possessions.

As quickly as he could, Frank immediately threw four books, his passport, a stack of hundred dollar bills and a battered old photo of his deceased nephew into his duffel bag. He then went into his dingy kitchen and opened up his fridge. The only things within it were a gallon of milk, a big jug of grape juice and half of a watermelon.

He then grabbed a glass from a dirty cabinet and quickly poured himself a cup full of juice. As he consumed his drink, he noticed out of the corner of his eye, a mouse which scurried as quickly as it had come under his stove.

"Ahhhh," he exhaled in satisfaction as he finished his glass.

He then proceeded into his bedroom to search for something.

After minutes of going through different drawers, he finally found what it was that he had been searching for. A black notepad that was labeled *'FRANK PLANS'* was then opened as he started turning its pages…

Some time had passed when Matthews' finger abruptly came across a telephone number of a man circled in red marker.

Upon dialing it, Matthews walked into the living room and waited. Within seconds, a man with a slight Cuban accent finally picked up.

"Hello?" he said.

"Señor Henriquez," said Matthews.

"Yes, speaking," he replied suspiciously.

"It's me, Frank," said Matthews.

"Primo, cómo esta?" he asked in a much lighter tone.

"Estoy okay," said Frank as he continuously scanned all aspects of his dirty apartment, before peeking out of the blinds of his window.

The man on the other line chuckled as he heard the Spanglish that Frank had spoken.

"Que pasa? You okay?" he asked.

"I won't be if I stay here," replied Frank.

"Remember that case that I told you about?" he added.

"Si," replied Señor Henriquez.

"Well, they're close to figuring out that it was me and so I need to get the hell out of here!"

"Okay, okay. When are you coming?" asked Henriquez.

"Tomorrow morning."

"So soon?"

"Didn't you hear what I fu—"

Matthews somehow found a way to suppress his simmering temper. The man was definitely his only way out of the country.

"Look, I'm coming okay? I'm going to buy a ticket for a flight after midnight. I don't care if it even costs me a grand, I'm doing it."

"Okay, okay," said Señor Henriquez again. "Just let me know when you land. I have my boys who are supposed to get two keys for me. I'll make sure that they're at the airport to pick you up as well."

"Thank you," said Frank.

"Adios, amigo. I see you soon," he said in his Cuban accent.

Frank quickly hung up. He was on edge and hoped that he had no more setbacks going forward. He then turned on his Dell PC and scoured the internet for one-way flight tickets to the Caribbean. After booking his flight and printing out the ticket and confirmation receipt, he then went into his bedroom and looked out of that window.

There were children playing tag on one end of the corner and drug-dealers selling weight on the other.

"No more bullshit," he thought aloud.

He would finally be leaving his poverty stricken neighborhood behind forever.

In that precise moment, Matthews' Nextel dispatcher began to bleep.

As he looked down at his phone, he bothered not to answer and threw it right out of the window. He watched the phone fall from where he stood before it shattered into many pieces upon hitting the concrete ground.

As he removed himself away from the window, he went into his duffel to make sure everything was in place when his house phone started to ring. It was now nine p.m. and Frank was paranoid about taking any calls. The fact that he was leaving forever, none of it mattered to him anymore.

As he watched the phone ring numerous amounts of times before letting it go to voicemail, a beep then sounded as he heard a voice that he was all too familiar with.

"Matthews! Where are you? It's me James," said the captain.

"Listen, Lane wanted me to keep this quiet until the morning but since you're lead of homicide, I thought that I'd inform you.

It looks as if the Fisher case isn't dead after all. She's discovered some intriguing developments and she'd like to share them with all of us tomorrow. I need you to be at the precinct, first thing," he said before hanging up and finishing his message.

This was the news he had been waiting for. Miss valedictorian also known as detective Lane had solved the puzzle and planned on exposing him in front of the entire 23rd precinct.

"Smart girl," he thought.

"But not smart enough. A real player of the game doesn't play their cards all out in the open like that," he said to himself before letting out a slight chuckle.

Although it was only 9:30p.m., Matthews didn't want to take any chances as he made strides to exit his apartment.

Upon entering his car, he kicked on the engine and made his way to John F. Kennedy International airport in Queens.

At approximately midnight, he boarded his plane with just a single suitcase and duffle bag as he forever left Brooklyn and the United States of America all together.

Exactly a week later, Matthews was unfolding a beach chair while wearing swimming trunks, a tank-top and as well as shades. He then lied down upon the chair as he soaked up the glorious sun and sipped on a margarita. As he read a newspaper from the four letter island that he newly inhabited, he happily watched four beautiful women walk on by in skimpy bikinis as they spoke in Spanish at a frantic pace.

"If only it was 1972," he said as he took another sip of his drink.

After what seemed like two hours, it suddenly hit Frank that Valentine's Day was upon him as he had now been away from the states for exactly a year. Not that he cared or anything, but he couldn't help but wonder about the status of everyone back in Brooklyn. Had they gone on a notorious hunt throughout the country searching for him? Had Lane really planned on exposing him? How had Luke Fisher felt once he was told the truth about his brother's murder? A sudden idea came to him as he quickly went into his pocket and pulled out a little black book.

On the inside of the cover marked the words, **Matt Frank: "FRANKLY TWISTED"**

He then turned some pages until he found a section that was left totally blank. He took one good sip of his margarita before his pen and pad finally met the page:

'Let me make this clear. Quite frankly, I've been a twisted individual for as long as I can remember…But just know that behind every method, there is a reason to its madness…'

THE END

Pilot:

"Gordon's Lost Files"

It's February 17th, 2013. Three days after Valentine's Day and trust me when I say there's no love found here. We may have re-elected President Obama, but crimes never seem to cease in the harsh realities of America, especially in Brooklyn, New York. I have since stepped down as head of the 23rd precinct due to my ever increasing age.

As hard as it is to believe, I am now seventy-five and living out the rest of my life in peace. Former detective Alvin Alvin has succeeded and replaced me as Captain of Parkside Avenue's unit.

I think it's great that detective Alvin has become my successor. He is now 51 and in my eyes, responsible and competent enough to handle such duties. However, before we get on to that, I'd like to handle the real course of business here.

This day marks the 10th anniversary of Frank Matthews' escape. And within this time that I've had off, I brought back a crate of files from the precinct to my house that were once lost during that time of importance.

As I was digging through the files, I came across many clues and interesting events that I never took into consideration. One, being the biggest mistake as I gave Frank Matthews the "Ron Mercer" case during our crossfires task at 59th and Columbus. In time, you, the reader, will be able to delve into three specific cases that make up the complexity of the lost files.

First, detective Lane will give you her accounts of life as a newly promoted female detective and how being a woman has plagued and hindered her work.

Furthermore, she will exhibit grit, determination and skill that promoted her to lead detective within the burglary unit to begin with. Then, you will be introduced to the crossfire criminals through the meanings of a case that takes place a year before the subway show down. Lastly, in an assignment I regret handing out (as previously stated) Detective Matthews will exhibit his cruel tendencies as he murders Jake Fisher and disposes of Ron Mercer. This account will be handled by newly appointed captain Alvin Alvin. Now my question to you the readers is are you ready? There's a lot of stuff that goes on within these files that you must submit your undivided attention to. And so, I now present to you frankly TWISTED: THE LOST FILES…

About The Illustrator

Alton Taylor is a self-employed cartoonist/illustrator/author and has Bruce Timm and as well as Darwyn Cooke to thank for his influences. During his time spent at Queensborough Community College in Bayside, New York as a Fine & Performing Arts major, it was there where he met Founder/Publisher/Author of Flowered Concrete, Kevin Anglade, (Kevin Eleven) who discovered Alton's works on his website and later asked him to be a part of the small publishing press. Through Flowered Concrete and with Anglade's help, Taylor has published two books, his first called, *The Serpent Samurai*, a short book about a fallen warrior in medieval Japan and also a book by the name of *You & I*, which is a ten page art book filled with illustrations of romance and as well as poetic lines that pertain to love. Recently, as of October 2014, Taylor published his first sketchbook through his own drawing freelance art company called drawing realm presents: *GENESIS*. Along with his good friend and colleague, Kevin Anglade, the artist also featured on NBC's final season of *The Debrief with David Ushery* in May of 2014. As an artist, he one day dreams of meeting and working with his two influences stated above and also doing a CD cover design for his favorite noise-rock/indie electronica band called, HEALTH. The illustrator/author is now currently working on his third book and first full-length, called *Yelloworld*, a noir crime thriller, which is expected for publication early 2016.

About The Author

Kevin Eleven, whose real name is Kevin Anglade, was raised in the Queens borough section of New York City. He published his debut novel *Tales of the 23RD PRECINCT* through his indie press, Flowered Concrete in January of 2013. In spring 2014, he graduated from Brooklyn College with a BA in English while concentrating in literature. Also, he was featured on NBC's final season of *The Debrief with David Ushery* as he spoke upon his indie press, Flowered Concrete, and its endeavors as an up-and-coming small publisher. In 2015, his latest work, frankly TWISTED: the lost files placed first in the Mystery/Thriller category and won Best Fiction Award by a select panel of literary judges at Urban Literary Agency. When not writing or fulfilling Flowered Concrete related duties, the author likes spending his down time by reading, playing basketball, listening to music, and performing poetry at lounges/cafes throughout NYC. He often dreams about being one of the most revered as well as acclaimed writers to ever endure and live within the realms of the twenty-first century.

Also by <u>Flowered Concrete</u>

Kevin Eleven's:

"Tales of the 23RD PRECINCT"

"motown, BLUES"

"pReSSuREd": aNotHeR hoOd sToRy

Alton Taylor's:

"The Serpent Samurai"

"You & I"

Coming SOON!

"Yelloworld" by Alton Taylor

Visit our official website at www.floweredconcrete.net to purchase our books or find out more info regarding Flowered Concrete related news, our latest titles, and also readings, signings and events in your area.

Be sure to re-read "Tales of the 23rd PRECINCT" or purchase a copy if you have yet to read it because this book serves as its prequel. Once you have done that, you'll most certainly be up to date and ready to read the third and final story within the "Tales of the 23rd Trilogy".

Book three is *Mercy for Murder: In Brooklyn...*

Bonus Info

Can't get enough of the "frankly TWISTED" fun?! Be sure to check out *frankly TWISTED: The Procedural*, an all-new handbook guide that will enlighten readers on everything consisting of the "Tales of the 23rd Trilogy" which includes character bios, (dossiers) episode tidbits, settings, a timeline, themes, the fictional Brooklyn Police Department, and symbols surrounding the world of Brooklyn's own, *23rd precinct*. Visit www.floweredconcrete.net and download the file under the Book Extra's section.

All that you have to do is click upon frankly TWISTED: The Procedural's artwork and experience all of the fun. You can also purchase the procedural in its physical form as a collector's item on special occasions such as holidays, and anniversaries.

Praise for frankly TWISTED

"This book is an excellent reminder that we cannot forget to continue to fight for justice in our own towns."

- *Urban Literary Agency*

"If you have read Tales of the 23rd Precinct and enjoyed it, frankly TWISTED wraps up things nicely (which is why I'm intrigued as to what could happen in the next book), and is an interesting novel. Overall, this book is a solid 3.5 stars."

- Analee S. of *Book Snacks Blog*

"Kevin Eleven's writing is totally well-suited for this style of literature, I'm going to give frankly TWISTED: the lost files 3.5 stars out of 5 for keeping me intrigued from start to finish and having a genuinely gripping story within it."

- Amanda O'Hara of *The Darling Bookworm*

"frankly TWISTED is not the latest Nancy Drew, yet, it's coming scarily close. I would recommend this book to anyone looking for easy reading, or just to simply gain pleasure from a book."

- Lydia Wilkins of *Mademoiselle Books*

"My first thought when reading this book is how much it feels like a TV series. The chapters are episodes and the cases within them are solved by the time the imagined credits role. Similarly, throughout every episode there are hints of something bigger that builds and builds until we get to the season finale."

- Claudia F. Vogt of *Bernie & Books*

""frankly TWISTED": the lost files, is one of the best new literature masterpieces readers will read this summer."

- Danielle Urban of *Universal Creativity Inc.*

www.ingramcontent.com/pod-product-compliance
Lightning Source LLC
Chambersburg PA
CBHW021153130626
46554CB00005B/1800